BLAST FROM THE PAST

Kinky Friedman lives in a little green trailer in a little green valley deep in the heart of Texas. There are about ten million imaginary horses in the valley and quite often they gallop around Kinky's trailer, encircling the author in a terrible, ever-tightening carousel of death. Even as the hooves are pounding around him in the darkest night, one can hear, almost in counterpoint, the frail, consumptive, ascetic novelist tip-tip-tapping away on the last typewriter in Texas. In such fashion he has turned out eleven novels including *Roadkill, The Love Song of J. Edgar Hoover, God Bless John Wayne, Armadillos & Old Lace* and *Elvis, Jesus and Coca-Cola.* Two cats, Dr Scat and Lady Argyle, a pet armadillo called Dilly, and a small black dog named Mr Magoo can sometimes be found sleeping with Kinky in his narrow, monastic, Father Damien-like bed.

by the same author

GREENWICH KILLING TIME

WHEN THE CAT'S AWAY

FREQUENT FLYER

MUSICAL CHAIRS

ELVIS, JESUS & COCA-COLA

ARMADILLOS AND OLD LACE

GOD BLESS JOHN WAYNE

THE LOVE SONG OF J. EDGAR HOOVER

A CASE OF LONE STAR

ROADKILL

Blast from the Past

KINKY FRIEDMAN

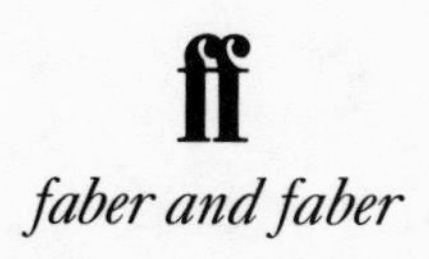

faber and faber

First published in the United States in 1998 by Simon & Schuster
First published in the United Kingdom in 1998
by Faber and Faber Limited
3 Queen Square London WC1N 3AU

Printed in England by Clays Ltd, St Ives plc

A CIP record for this book
is available from the British Library

ISBN 0-571-19652-7

2 4 6 8 10 9 7 5 3 1

Acknowledgments

The author would like to thank all of the people authors usually like to thank. First of all, of course, my wonderful wife. Unfortunately, she passed away early this morning. I had to kill her and take her to my Lord. She never really appreciated my work anyway. She didn't realize I could be looking out a window and still be working hard thinking up scenes for a book that was obviously ghost-written by an idiot-savant masturbating like a monkey in a mental hospital. I've never met the guy, but whoever ghost-writes these books is a genius. Hell, it's hard enough just writing the acknowledgments.

The author would like to thank Charles Bukowski, Jesus Christ, and Scrooge McDuck for their encouragement and unflagging support. You guys were great! I'd also like to thank my editor, Chuck Adams, for taking invaluable time away from his other editing project, *Black Yachtsmen I Have Known*.

Of special note, the author would like to thank his mother and father, Min and Tom Friedman, for conceiving him in Casper, Wyoming, and providing him with a happy childhood, which, of course, as we all know, is the worst possible preparation for life. Tom has always been there for me and I probably hold my mother's hand more than I know. Min's in heaven now, if there is such a place, along with Cuddles, Kacey Cohen, Tom Baker, John Morgan, Earl

Buckelew, and practically everybody else I love and whom, no doubt, I will be happily joining as soon as I finish these acknowledgments.

Steve Rambam was the technical consultant for this book as well as coming up with the title, Blast from the Past. Don Imus has stood by me for so long that I'm thinking about mounting him (not sexually). My sister Marcie read the manuscript and promptly hung herself. Max Swafford, who I wish had hung himself, typed the manuscript onto the computer, which I still refuse to touch because, like the Unabomber, I believe that every time you use it it takes away a little piece of your soul and increases the possibility of your opening up Mr. Kinky's Nail Boutique in Paris, Texas.

I would like to have thanked my agent, Esther "Lobster" Newberg, but instead, I've dedicated the book to her in hopes that she'll work harder. Some people think that I should work harder, too, but I don't want to rupture myself toting around tedious tissues of horseshit Torah portions all over the place. I have to conserve my energy so I can thank Carolyn Reidy, David Rosenthal, Cheryl Weinstein, Ted Landry, Christine Saunders, and all the other fine folks at Simon & Schuster.

My deepest gratitude also goes to Dr. Charles Ansell for contributing the word "petzel", which means "diminutive penis" in Yiddish. My thanks extend as well to Willis Hoover for providing Jesus's last words from the New Testament. As Hoover points out: "If it ain't King James, it ain't Bible."

Finally, I'd like to thank my reluctant muse, Stephanie DuPont, whom I recently asked if she'd go on a honeymoon trip with me to Easter Island. "Yes," she said, "but how will they get my casket on the plane?"

And now I have to kill everybody on the elevator.

Kinky Friedman, Jewfish Bayou, January 1, 1953

This book is dedicated
to my friend and agent
Esther “Lobster” Newberg

Blast from the Past

In my nostrils still lives the breath of flowers that perished twenty years ago.

Mark Twain, remembering his visit to Hawaii

PART ONE The Present Tense

Surely I come quickly.

Jesus's last words, Book of Revelation 22:20

1

Call me Kinky.

It's not my true Christian name, of course, but then, I'm not a true Christian. If you don't believe me, maybe I can sell you the bridge of my nose. For, indeed, what true Christian, with Sunday-morning church bells ringing cacophonously all around him, would prefer sitting in a cold, drafty loft one floor below a lesbian dance class, puffing a cigar, sipping an espresso, and playing chess with a cat? It was a slow game, but I'd seen slower.

"Are you going to make a move," I said to the cat, "or are you just going to sit there?"

The cat, of course, said nothing. Nor did she deign to make a move. She was one of that maddening breed of finicky, meticulously conservative players who now and again cause you to want to reach across the table and yank their whiskers. There are, however, very few female chess players of merit in this world. If you have the good fortune to stumble across one, you always make allowances.

Outside the kitchen window winter had entirely enveloped the city, white as Rosinante, cold as the ashes of Jean Harlow's honeymoon. Harry Houdini's ghost, apparently, had placed Vandam Street under a trance. For a moment it seemed like it could be any other city block along the parade route of life's charade. For a moment it almost made a country singer-turned-private investigator wonder if he could solve the mystery of what in the hell he was doing here in the first place.

One of the many things New York City is not conducive to is a peaceful game of chess. Now, as the cat and I stared silently at the board, the small wooden pieces dissolving dreamily into dear, dead, dusty friends, a new and extremely unpleasant noise intruded itself upon the already tedious clamor of the church bells. A horn was honking in a somewhat irregular series of very loud, very long blasts. Like love, like trouble, like the extended stay of a hideous housepest, just when you thought it was over for good, it started up again.

"That tears it," I said to the cat. "I doubt whether even Van Gogh could masturbate under these conditions. However, through the power of Sherlockian deductive reasoning, I will now describe for you the nature of the villain who is creating such a repellent racket."

The cat looked at me with traffic-light eyes. Ever-changing. Now yellow. Now green. Now blinking, it seemed to me, somewhat doubtfully.

"The horn itself does not seem to have the dull, pedestrian timbre of the average horn on the average four-wheeled penis that speeds along the streets and sometimes the sidewalks of

New York. Nor does it have the deep, resonant foghorn quality of a large vehicle—for instance, a garbage truck. Today being Sunday, we can exclude garbage trucks altogether. You can't count on them to pick up the trash on any day, but on Sunday, like all good little church-workers, the garbage trucks rest. Unfortunately, most of them like to rest on Vandam Street."

The cat looked at me with pity in her eyes. I ignored her gaze and continued my calm, scientific analysis. Sherlockian deduction leaves no room for human emotions. Just as I was starting to speak the horn, an earsplitting, high-pitched, endless urban fart, sounded again.

"Twenty-seven seconds," I said. "Quite a singular occurrence if I'm not mistaken. The four-wheeled penis is no doubt new, expensive, and probably of foreign manufacture. Very likely driven by a detestable young person who obviously is not of a religious bent. The driver could not be incapacitated. Surely he'd have been mugged or assisted by this time, so an epileptic seizure or heart attack is out of the question. We can also rule out an electronic alarm on a parked four-wheeled penis. The fartings are too sustained and at intervals of too much irregularity. That last blast was thirteen seconds."

The cat stared at me very possibly in the same uncomprehending way Van Gogh's cat had stared at him during the last years of his life, when the two of them had shared the same padded cell in Dr. Gachet's mental hospital. Like Van Gogh's cat, my cat probably thought I belonged in wig city as well. He *must* be crazy, she no doubt figured. Why else would anybody become obsessed with a car honking out on the street when they could be playing chess with a cat? Sherlockian dictum, of course, places very little stock in the whimsical wanderings of females or cats in general.

"Since it is Sunday and the traffic is light, the young woman in the foreign car is most likely trying to get the attention of someone in an upstairs loft or apartment not equipped with an intercom or buzzer to let her into the building."

At this point I got up from my chair and began pacing the living room of the loft. Back and forth I paced, puffing the cigar, studiously avoiding getting too close to the Vandam-side windows. My pacing was punctuated at intermittent intervals by extended, highly irritating horn blasts.

"How do I know it's a woman, you ask?" I said rhetorically to the cat, as I stopped pacing and turned dramatically toward the kitchen table.

Much to my Cheshire chagrin, the cat was now lying on its back on the table, sound asleep with all four paws in the air. When you blind the world with science there will always be those perverse enough to close their eyes. Nonetheless, I plodded on, shouting at the slumbering feline like a madman in a play.

"How do I know it's a woman behind the wheel? Because a man hits the horn in a threatening, rhythmic, staccato fashion, like a native of the Congo beating on his bongo. A similarly highly agitato woman takes a quite different approach. She leans on the horn with her whole neurotic, love-scarred life. So a young woman in an expensive foreign car is making this ungodly commotion on the very day that most of the world regards as God's day of rest. Fortunately, we are not most of the world."

Ready to test my powers of Sherlockian deductive reasoning, I gently scooped up the mildly protesting cat and together we walked to the kitchen window. I set the cat, who was now quite peeved, on the windowsill, and boldly gazed directly down on Vandam Street.

A shiny black Porsche with a vanity license plate that read EXCESS was parked just to the left of the building. As I opened the window, a young, blond, drop-dead-gorgeous woman unfolded her long legs and stepped out of the Porsche. I'd remembered reading in my *National Enquirer* that Jerry Seinfeld owned twelve Porsches. That was the definition of pathetic, I recalled thinking at the time. I didn't even like people who drove *one* Porsche. Of course, there are exceptions to every rule and I was gawking at one of them now.

As the young woman disdainfully skirted a parked garbage truck, two small dogs on leashes became visible to the cat and myself. A brief moue of distaste crossed the countenance of the cat. I watched the dogs, the red high-heels, the expensive-looking leather briefcase she carried, and the cocksure, sensuous way she carried everything else about her. There was no mistaking it. She was very familiar-looking. Of course, you never completely forget someone who's broken your heart.

Now the dogs were yipping and yapping. Now the snowflakes were falling gently upon her red stilettoes. Now she was laughing carelessly and smiling a stunning snow-blind smile that sailed up four stories right into my unfurnished eyes. Now, like a man in a trance, I walked to the refrigerator, picked up the little Negro puppet head from its perch on top. It had a colorful parachute attached to it and the key to the building in its smiling, stoic mouth. I walked back to the window again and looked down at the beautiful woman below. A young girl, really. Almost kindred spirits we were. The only difference between us was that she loved a little black Porsche and I loved a little black puppet head.

"Come on, hummingbird dick!" she screamed. "Throw down that sick little puppet head."

"Someday you'll eat those words," I shouted, continuing to hold the cheerful little puppet head in the palm of my hand. "And, by the way, it's *Mister* Hummingbird Dick to you."

"Okay," she said, starting to shiver a bit, "*Mister* Hummingbird Dick."

She'd gotten rid of the smile, I noticed, and the snowflakes were building little castles in her long blond hair. Later, I would remember her that way. Standing there like an angry statue waiting for me to throw her the key to my heart.

I threw down the puppet head, she caught it in a rapacious grip, and soon the lady and the two little dogs had disappeared inside the building. I shut the window and puffed on the cigar thoughtfully. I watched a purple plume of cigar smoke traveling tentatively upward toward the lesbian dance class. I watched a careless canopy of snowflakes drifting downward onto the little black Porsche.

The cat sat on the windowsill watching the snow. I stood a little behind her, watching the cat watching the snow. Without touching any pieces we both knew that another chess game had begun.

"Actually," I said, "it's *Lord* Hummingbird Dick."

The cat, of course, said nothing.

2

The freight elevator in the lonely little lobby was slow, but after about an hour I was starting to get worried. For one thing, I didn't want her running off with the puppet head. Many a time it'd provided that special little smile that's sometimes just enough to keep you from hanging yourself from the shower rod. Quite often, when your spirits are low, a little head is all you really need.

But there was nothing to worry about, I figured. More than likely she was just taking her time moving back into her old apartment upstairs. I didn't want to give her the satisfaction of calling her or knocking on her door just to find out that she was across the hall trading recipes with Winnie Katz and her lesbian dance class. She could write, she could call, she could just forget it all. I hadn't heard a word from her in many months, so an hour or two more wasn't going to take another little piece out of Janis Joplin's heart.

"You remember Stephanie DuPont, of course," I said to the

cat. "Of course, of course, my kingdom for a Porsche. About three or four lives ago she went down to Florida with me and a treasure map, searching for Al Capone's hidden fortune. She and the map decided to stay down there. I decided to come back."

The cat made a little show of stretching and yawning but at least managed this time to stay awake. After all, it was an old story. Boy meets girl. Girl uses boy to help lead her to buried treasure. When treasure isn't found girl tells boy to bug out for the dugout. Happens every day in America and even some developing countries.

"You may not remember Stephanie too well, but I know you remember her two adorable little dogs, Pyramus and Thisbe. Now let me see, Pyramus was the cuddly little Yorkshire terrier, I think. Or was Thisbe the Yorkie? No, Thisbe was the precious little Maltese. I'm pretty sure of that—"

I'd been watching the cat's eyes, and something in there had definitely changed. They'd gone from wishing wells to fires of hell in less than the time it takes to catch a rat in New York.

"I *thought* you'd remember the time those two little boogers visited us here at our humble loft. As I recall there was a bit of a tension convention between Pyramus and Thisbe and yourself. You were a little weak in the horsepitality department, I believe. But I can understand that. Sometimes I feel that way about Stephanie DuPont."

I walked over to the counter and poured a strong bolt of Jameson Irish Whiskey into the old bull's horn. Time for brunch. I started to give a silent toast to the puppet head, but then I realized it wasn't there. The top of the refrigerator looked as empty as Wall Street on Yom Kippur. I offered a little salute to the puppet head anyway.

"To fallen comrades," I said.

Then I killed the shot. Drinking in the morning, according to the experts, is a sure sign of depression in a person. I understand their narrow logic, of course, but I see having a drink in the morning as a necessary medicinal bridge. In other words, before you can need something to help you make it through the night you've got to get there first. The psychological term we like to use for this type of depression is African-American Puppet Head Post-Partum.

Well, I figured, I'd just have to deal with it. Without the puppet head, there just wouldn't be anyone ever coming into the loft again. That was fine with me and probably even finer with the cat. No more fair-weather friends vampirizing your spirits and your spirit. No more housepests hanging around through the eight nights of Chanukah, exchanging nothing but their unwanted presence. No more lovers breaking your heart, busting your balls, bitching about your belching, and letting down your toilet seats and your dreams. It'd be a lonely, monastic existence, of course, for the cat and myself. But somehow, I suspected, we'd manage. After all, it was hardly the functionality of the puppet head I would miss; it was its humanity.

I only hoped that if I had to go puppet headless for a while it wouldn't threaten my growing success as a private investigator. The past few years particularly, while certainly not a major financial pleasure for the Kinkster, had at least established my reputation in the city as a canny, crepuscular, cat-loving crime-solver. I'd found a few cats and a few people and a few skeletons in the closet and now I was trying to find a way not to turn into a skeleton myself, because none of my last three cases had brought in any bucks. My erstwhile Dr. Watson, Larry "Ratso" Sloman, still waiting to inherit slightly under fifty-seven million dollars from his birth mother's estate, which I helped him locate, had steadfastly kept me still waiting to inherit his bill. Likewise, in a case my reporter friend Mike McGovern had dubbed "The Love Song of J. Edgar Hoover," a chain of cowboy logic had led Stephanie DuPont and myself to Florida where we almost discovered Al Capone's long-lusted-after buried treasure. But the deeper we dug the shallower became our trust in each other, until at last we'd managed to bury what was left of our friendship in a similarly shallow grave.

In the brokenhearted, dispirited down time that followed Florida, my PI pal Rambam and I rounded up the culprit in a fairly murderous little matter surrounding America's last living folk hero, Willie Nelson. Subsequently, I was able to locate the reclusive redhead who himself had gone into hiding for reasons that I cannot divulge in this family newspaper. Nelson did not especially appreciate being found and, though he's back on the road again, the two of us, while remaining spiritually close, have maintained a somewhat lesser degree of social intercourse and certainly no sexual intercourse. Indeed, I haven't been involved in sexual intercourse with anyone for quite a while now and I hate to think of all that hummingbird semen going to waste. If the truth be told, because of a rather fortunate gene pool, I have a large penis like Ernest Hemingway, not a small penis like F. Scott Fitzgerald. Now the only matter I still have to resolve is whether I want to blow my fucking brains out or merely drink myself to death.

So, the net result of several years of difficult and daunting detective work has been that Ratso's hardly speaking to me, Willie's barely singing to me, and my rather rocky, acerbic relationship with Stephanie has gone from a romantic, quixotic dream to a tedious, ubiquitous nightmare. The field of amateur detective work, however, is often fallow, often fraught with frightfully forbidden fruit from which the detective himself often reaps a harvest of hatred. This is because everyone says they want the truth, but once the truth is known, few, if any, want to deal with it. Sometimes not even the investigator himself. A couple more successes like the ones I'd recently had, I figured, and the cat and I would be about ready for a time-share arrangement in Van Gogh's old padded cell.

Such were my deep, metaphysical thoughts as Sunday morning scuttled along into Sunday afternoon much in the manner of a wayward, oblivious dung beetle. I was smoking another cigar, drinking another shot of Jameson's, and watching the black and white football players tump over on my old black and white television set when the lesbian dance class kicked into high gear overhead and the two red telephones on opposite sides of the desk sprang to life at the same time. This was not surprising, really, because they were both connected to the same line. It was also not surprising to see the cat do a double back flip because she was sleeping precisely midway between the two phones.

"My, my," I said, "suddenly the loft has become an Africanized beehive of activity."

The cat, of course, said nothing. She sat on the desk and licked lazily at her paw, pretending the embarrassing incident hadn't happened at all. The ability to laugh at one's self is noticeably absent in virtually all cats and also in the vast majority of adult human beings. In human beings, we call this condition by its clinical name: late-blooming serious. In cats, of course, it is not a condition at all; it is merely the way of their people.

I took a few peaceful puffs on the cigar to settle my nerves and then picked up the blower on the left.

"Start talkin'," I said.

"Hummingbird dick."

"Ah, my frail little five-foot-eleven Aryan flower. So nice of you to call now that you're back in the city."

"I've lost my key to the building, Hebe. Otherwise, I would've—Pyramus! Thisbe! Stop chewing on that puppet head—"

"What?"

"Relax, nerd. I've taken it away from them."

"Well, drop it off sometime on your way down. By the way, sorry things didn't work out for you in Florida."

"What makes you think things didn't work out, fuckbrain?"

"Well, I mean, you came back—"

"So did John Travolta, but of course, he owes it all to Scientology. And I don't recall him bringing you any bucks."

"Bucks?"

"No, not the little deer with the little antlers that you big, brave Texans blow away every year—"

"Not *all* Texans—"

"I'm talkin' cash, dickhead. Your share of the cash. A deal's a deal. I'm a girl who keeps her word."

"Well—"

"What's the matter with you? Are you brain dead? This is the part where you're supposed to say 'How much?'"

"Okay. How much?"

"Your take is seven."

"Seven dollars doesn't go as far as it used to."

"Try seven *million* dollars."

3

It isn't every day you can leap sideways out of bed, play a little chess with the cat, then walk upstairs and come back down with seven million dollars. This is the kind of experience, in fact, that can ruin a man's life. I was very eager to give it a try. Of course, before you ruin your life it goes without saying that first you have to have one. And you don't want to waste your life, if, indeed, you think you may have one, by endlessly wondering whether or not you do. You can just let all the youthful moralistic nerds of the world figure it out for you, most of whom, no doubt, are too young and too chock-full of life to realize that Lenny Bruce died for their sins. They probably think Jesus played racquetball. They don't understand that while all of us wonderful Americans are entitled to the pursuit of happiness, none of us is ever going to catch up with it. We of Nike Village are destined to discover one day that the only shards of true happiness we are ever likely to find shall lie in the pursuit and not in the happiness. Knowing all this crap, why in the hell should I run up and down a flight of stairs just to collect seven million dollars from some youthful moralistic nerd who took three showers a day and thought I should get a life?

Of course, if you stopped to think about it, you could live pretty good on seven million dollars. You could move to Beverly Hills, buy one of those big Hum-Vee Desert Storm vehicles, and drive to get cappuccino every morning. But that's been done. Any way you looked at it, walking up the stairs would certainly be an expensive proposition. You also just might find yourself belly-up in the coin of the spirit department.

"Money may buy you a fine dog," I said to the cat, "but only love can make it wag its tail."

For a myriad of reasons, the cat did not appear to appreciate this bit of folksy sentiment. For one thing, she'd heard it many times. For another, she didn't want anyone buying any kind of dog, whether it wagged its tail or bit John Steinbeck in the ass. Probably more important, the cat somehow cosmically knew that biting the bullet now wasn't going to keep you from putting it in your head later, like Richard Cory, and she managed to convey this abstract, existential notion cats have done throughout history by merely looking at the human being with pity in her eyes. There are a myriad of reasons, of course, for any cat to look at any human being with pity in its eyes, but first and foremost amongst these would be if the person is a posturing, pontificating, middle-aged, amateur private investigator who's known from the very beginning that nothing's going to stop him from passing GO and collecting seven million dollars.

Thus it was, that fateful Sunday afternoon in the year of our Lord 1997, that I closed the door of the loft, leaving the cat in charge, and with mildly metaphysical tread began the step-by-step odyssey, quite simultaneously, both into the future and into the past. My interest was to come back down the stairs with seven million dollars and a little Negro puppet head, but unfortunately, as I was rounding the turn heading for the Valhalla that was Stephanie DuPont's upstairs apartment, something unpleasant happened to my own head. It felt like someone had stepped out of an old grainy black and white movie and sapped me. Then Ted Turner had colorized the movie and a rainbow coalition of pain went reeling out of control across the landscape of my gray matter department. Then, as they say in Hollywood, everything happened at once.

Suddenly, I was Alice falling through the looking glass. Suddenly, I was Dorothy falling through the Oz-hole of Kansas. Suddenly, I was everyone who'd ever been mugged in New York. I had the strange sensation of traveling through space and time, falling backward, backward, through O-rings and hula hoops and Richard Nixon's eyes. How far backward I could not say. All I knew was that somebody'd done a pretty damn thorough job of punching my ticket.

Just before I closed my eyes a door opened. In the doorway, dressed in radiant white, stood Stephanie DuPont. Next to her was the little black puppet head, but this time an entire human body seemed attached. And the last thing I remember was the very strangest thing of all.

The puppet head was not smiling.

PART TWO The Past Imperfect

Not a long time—but a good time.

Kacey Cohen

4

Andy Gibb was singing "I Just Want to Be Your Everything" when there came a knocking at the door. I couldn't answer it. I was right in the middle of someone. I was also right in the middle of Ratso's old, decrepit couch. The one with the skid marks on it. After a long night of Peruvian marching powder, I'd come in for an instrument landing, apparently, at Ratso's old place on Prince Street in SoHo. The apartment was in its usual state of disarray. About seven hundred hockey sticks were leaning precariously against one wall. Against another were stacked over ten thousand books, all dealing with either Jesus, Hitler, or Bob Dylan. The polar bear's head was mounted on the wall above the couch and now seemed to be staring balefully down at me. Folksinger Phil Ochs and rock guitarist Michael Bloomfield had both occupied the couch prior to me, of course, and subsequently both had stepped on a rainbow and gone to Jesus, which was hardly reassuring to the Kinkster at a time like this.

And the someone I was right in the middle of? She was a redhead. A true redhead, I'd come to find out. I'd always been a sucker for redheads, just as Sherlock Holmes accused his latent-homosexual roommate, Dr. Watson, of being. Watson, of course, always referred to their hair coloring as "auburn." But that was a long time ago, when the couch had no skid marks and Ratso had no books or hockey sticks and polar bears roamed free.

And the redhead? I now remembered I'd met her the night before at the Lone Star Cafe. I'd just finished the second set with my new band, the Shalom Retirement Village People. She'd swirled into the dressing room like a dangerous red tide. By mistake, she'd said. She'd been looking for somewhere to powder her nose. We'd told her she'd come to the right place. Now, one night later, here she was sandwiched between me and the skid marks. Who says rock 'n' roll relationships can't last?

What her game was it was too early to tell. What her name was doesn't matter to a tree. There are lots of redheads from North Carolina and lots of hard-luck country singers in this world, but it isn't every day that any two come together in quite such cosmic fashion. If you're keeping score at home, however, you'd probably like to know the name of the redhead. Of course, I can't tell you her real name. Something about protecting the innocent. Something about too soon. Something about too late. Something about who cares? Something about our very lives being over when we lose our dreams.

But I'll make a deal with you. Since inquiring minds want

to know, and since, when you're making love to somebody, you can't call them God all the time, I'll hold her close to my heart one more time and I'll find a name for the lady on Ratso's couch.

I'll call her Judy.

5

"Don't come!" said Judy. "Don't come!"

"I have to," said Ratso, standing in the doorway. "It's my apartment."

Ratso, it came to pass, was not alone. Neither, of course, was Judy. But social nuances of this sort, like two stark-naked, frenetically hosing people on his couch, never did give Ratso much pause. He waltzed right on in followed by Tom Baker and Jack Bramson. Bramson, at least, had the courtesy to go into the other room, but Ratso walked right over to the kitchen counter, set down a big bag from the Carnegie Deli, and, with Judy and me stuck together like two shivering dogs in the rain right under his nose, smiled mischievously as he removed four large corned beef sandwiches.

"Somebody'll have to split one," he said.

"Looks like somebody already has," said Baker.

I had to hand it to Judy. Either she hadn't noticed the intrusion or she was too far gone to care. Under the circumstances, I had no choice but to play along with her. It was a dirty job and I got to do it.

Ratso, for his part, busied himself in the kitchen organizing the sandwiches, needlessly banging pots and pans, shouting "Go, Kinkstah!" and singing a few snatches of "Someone's in the Kitchen with Dinah." But Tom Baker, troublemaker, was not so considerate. Baker, a talented actor often out of work but never out of wit, was probably my closest friend in the world. Now he was stomping around the living room pretending Judy and I weren't there and coming very close to getting up my sleeve. I wasn't, of course, wearing a shirt. Or anything else, for that matter. Judy, at least, was wearing me.

"Where's Pinky, I mean Blinky, I mean Finky, I mean Kinky?" said Baker. It was a personal mantra of his that he never failed to deliver and that never failed to irritate me.

"At least Bramson," I said, "had the good breeding to go into the other room."

"Bramson's got nothing on us," said Baker. "We've got some good breeding right here in this room."

"Don't stop," said Judy.

I had to admire her fortitude. Possibly she thought the interlopers would weary of their taunting and have the good sense to let the two lovers return to their previous, private little Garden of Eden. If that's what she thought, she was very much mistaken. With one arm, I pulled a weatherbeaten little quilt over the two of us, but it was going to take a fork lift to get Ratso and Baker out of here.

"What do I do with the extra sandwich?" Ratso shouted.

"You mean the one for Pinky, I mean Finky, I mean Stinky, I mean Kinky?" said Baker in loud, well-modulated, quasi-Shakespearean intonations.

"Don't stop," said Judy.

This, of course, was always good advice. If you ever really stopped to think about what you were doing you might very conceivably never do anything again. Not that it would make much difference. The paths of glory lead but to a stuffed polar bear's head. What this has to do with multiplying in front of the multitudes is an extremely hard, not to say seminal, Talmudic question that we need not enter into at this time. It is enough to say that if you were truly traveling along the paths of glory there'd be little chance of your leaving skid marks on Ratso's couch.

"Sooner or later," I said, "we have to stop. We'll have to eat, sleep, discuss off-Broadway—"

"Shut up and fuck me," she hissed like a biblical serpent.

Fortunately, by this time the Bakerman had wearied of his voyeuristic little game and retired into Ratso's medieval dumper, which was about the size of your nose. Ratso himself had also departed to join Bramson in the bedroom. Whatever they were discussing or doing back there was fine with me, as long as its running time outlasted Judy's. I felt like a participant-observer in a passion play where you know the climax is coming any moment. You can't just get up and walk out.

Soon even that unlikely opportunity was gone. And soon after that, I was glad that it was. She began trembling like a subway platform, muttering like the woman in *The Exorcist,* and, best of all, pulled me right along as a willing passenger through the tunnel of love and into the Flying Burrito Brothers' Gilded Palace of Sin. Coming together may not be quite everything it's cracked up to be but it is one of those things you can't do all by yourself. I've got to admit it felt so good that not only did it send my penis to Venus and cause the polar bear to smile at me, but it also caused me to begin invoking God's name more fervently than at any time since my bar mitzvah. Judy, for her part, was also busy invoking a name, but it didn't belong to God. It didn't even belong to me.

"Tim!" she shouted. "Oh, Tim!"

"Who's Tim?" said Ratso, coming back into the room.

It was a question I'd wondered about myself. But the answer, at least for the moment, was not forthcoming. Judy, with the tawdry quilt covering her body, lay back on the couch and fell asleep smiling up at the polar bear.

"Who's Tim?" Ratso asked again.

I looked down at Judy sleeping on the couch. I looked over at Ratso eating a corned beef sandwich. If there was an answer, it was certainly blowing in the wind.

"As Albert Einstein used to say," I told him, "'I don't know.'"

6

"I'd like you to meet Cleve Hattersley," said Bill Dick the next day as I walked into the Lone Star Cafe. Bill was the owner of the place; Cleve, so I was informed, was the new night manager; and I was there to rehearse with the band and to attempt to suck, fuck, or cajole a cash advance from a large, unfriendly woman wearing a green accountant's visor.

"Cleve will be working with you on your Sunday-night gigs," said Bill. "I hope we don't have any more problems like I heard about the other night."

"Just because they had to wheel me onstage in a gurney for the second show is nothing to worry about, Bill."

"Well," said Bill, "Cleve'll be here to see that everything goes smoothly. The show must go on. Right or wrong, Kinkster?"

"Right, Bill," I said.

"Cleve's a musician himself, Kinkster. Used to have a Texas band called—uh . . . what was the name of that band, Cleve?"

"Greezy Wheels," said Cleve.

"Oh sure," I said. "You guys were killer bee. Just a little ahead of your time."

"That's what I always heard about you guys," said Cleve. "The Texas Jewboys were great but just a little ahead of their time."

"It's not a bad thing to be ahead of your time," I said. "Jesus was ahead of his time but if you walk around with three nails long enough somebody's going to put you up for the night. Van Gogh was ahead of his time, too. That's why he cut his ear off. It's not true that he'd just returned from a Barry Antelope concert—"

"Well," said Bill Dick, "I'm sure you two have a lot in common and a lot to talk about, but right now I've got to meet this avant-garde Texas artist named Bob Wade. Calls himself Daddy-O. He's trying to talk me into putting some kind of giant lizard on the roof of the building. Craziest idea I ever heard. That'll happen over my dead body."

Bill Dick wandered off, and Cleve and I went over to the downstairs bar by the little stage to have a drink. The club was constructed in such a way that the bartender was the only person in the place who could see the show with an unobstructed view. The bartender was standing there now but all he could see was an empty stage and two guys who looked like they needed a charity shot.

"It's a cold afternoon," said Kurt, the bartender. "Why don't you guys have a drink on me?"

"Do we look that bad?" asked Cleve.

"Yes," said Kurt, who'd seen a lot of cool customers coming down from too much Peruvian marching powder and knew a frequent flyer when one landed at his bar. He poured us both a shot of something as we waited for my band to show up for the rehearsal.

"To a band that's definitely not ahead of its time," said Cleve.

"That's why I call them the Shalom Retirement Village People," I said.

We killed the shots, and mine tore off about half of my uvula on the way down. We waited.

"You know," I said to Cleve, "this club spits out night managers like sunflower seeds. The only one who's ever lasted is Lee Frazier and that's because he doesn't know he's a Negro."

"I've got a different approach," said Cleve.

"I'm sure you'll tell me what it is," I said. I was starting to like this guy in a perverse kind of way.

"Well," said Cleve, "if anyone gives me a hard time, I just kill 'em."

Cleve laughed. Kurt laughed. For the first time in over two hundred years, even I laughed. Cleve was a tall, thin guy with a long ponytail, a former hippie frustrated by the music business and by living life away from it. I knew the feeling myself and it wasn't very funny, which is probably why I laughed. There weren't too many other things to do.

"If they don't show up for this goddamn rehearsal pretty soon," I said, "I'd like for you to kill the Shalom Retirement Village People. How about another round of that snake-piss, Kurt?"

"Okay, but you'll have to pay for this one. Bill Dick monitors things with a microscope around here."

"Just put it on my tab," said Cleve.

"You don't have a tab," said Kurt. "You've only been working one day."

"I told you you'd have fun here, Cleve," I said. "I'd pay for the round myself, but I'm currently crashing on Ratso's couch."

"That pretty well says it all," said Kurt. "The next stop's free bean curd at the Hari Krishna Temple. Maybe you guys do deserve another one on the house."

He poured us both another generous shot. He poured himself one, too. I bummed a Lucky Strike from Cleve.

"To the future," I said. "What *is* this stuff, Kurt?"

"It's Jameson Irish Whiskey," he said. "What do you think?"

"Cuts the phlegm," I said.

We killed the shots. Then we sat at the bar for a while and waited for the Shalom Retirement Village People. I chain-bummed another Lucky from Cleve, smoked it, and field-stripped it, walked downstairs several times, once to urinate, and once to badger the large, unfriendly woman wearing the green accountant's visor. No bucks. No band. No joy.

Finally, by the time I was about ready to hang myself from a shower rod, the band arrived and began the rather laborious process of setting up on stage and tuning their instruments. They weren't the Texas Jewboys—they'd been on sabbatical for several years now—but they were a very damn good band, especially considering the fact that I often paid them in the coin of the spirit.

On drums was the great Howie Wyeth, formerly of Bob Dylan's band and arguably one of the best rock 'n' roll drummers in the world. On bass, which Bill Dick pronounced like the fish, was Buffalo, who snarted and farted on that instrument with the best of them. Buffalo was also one of the few cheerful bass players I have ever met. Maybe I needed two of whatever he was on. On keyboards was my old friend the talented Ron Slater, whom the Bakerman called the Late Great Slate. On harp was Sredni "Nigger-lips" Esquire who was often as hot as Paul Butterfield and often as soulful as Mickey Raphael. On guitar, mandolin, and fiddle was Larry Campbell, who could play every instrument known to man and was quite a good-looking young lad as well. Campbell was, in the words of Dylan Ferrero, the Jewboys' road manager, the band's main "butt draw."

We'd just started rehearsing when Cleve came over to the stage and motioned to me. We finished the song, which was a nice, upbeat version of "They Ain't Makin' Jews Like Jesus Anymore," and then I walked over to him.

"Phone call for you, Mr. Jolson," said Cleve.

"Is it a man, woman, or child?"

"None of the above," he said. "It's Ratso. Says it's urgent."

What could be urgent, I thought? My father and mother, Tom and Min, were in Austin, doing fine. My little sister, Marcie, was in high school, doing fine. My brother, Roger, was in Maryland, being a psychologist. Doing fine. And I was here in New York playing with the Shalom Retirement Village People, snorting about a gram of Irving Berlin's White Christmas a day, crashing on Ratso's couch, and doing a fairly good impersonation of Gram Parsons meets Lenny Bruce. Neither life had ended particularly well, I reflected. The date on Parsons's carton had expired at the age of twenty-six and his body had been stolen and burned at Joshua Tree in the

Mojave Desert. Bruce had OD'd on the toilet, like Judy Garland and Elvis, a mortal coda the Lord chooses to play only for his very brightest stars. Currently I could hear all of their angels calling to me with a great deal more intensity than Ratso. So what could be urgent?

I punched the flashing light on the blower by the bar.

"Start talkin'," I said.

"Judy's coming over. I think she wants to tell you who Tim is."

"After that, maybe she can tell me who I am."

"Never let a woman define you, Kinkstah," said Ratso. "She'll end up destroying you."

"Did anyone ever tell you you would've made a very good California pop psychologist?"

"I'm serious, Kinkstah. My whole life was destroyed by a woman and it started right on that very same couch."

"You're kidding."

"Where do you think those fucking skid marks came from, Kinkstah?"

7

Ratso hadn't charged Phil Ochs or Mike Bloomfield any rent to stay at his place and he wasn't charging me any now. Not that I was an ungrateful housepest, but you had to wonder at the wisdom of crashing on the same infamous couch that had discharged both music legends to Jesus almost immediately subsequent to their sojourn upon it. I didn't blame the couch, really. Nor did I hold Ratso in any way accountable. It was just that the spiritual ambience of the cluttered, congested, claustrophobic little apartment often made it extremely difficult for one to breathe or breed whilst in residence.

Compounding the problem was the indisputable fact that Ratso was the most anal-retentive human being on the entire planet, hoarding, saving, and collecting virtually every arcane form of detritus known to man. In fairness to Ratso, there did exist a certain utilitarian purpose to these endeavors: he quite often wore these strange collections on the feet, head, and torso of his body, constantly regaling anyone who would listen with detailed information regarding the apparel, such as how much each item cost or in which flea market he'd made the remarkable purchase.

Thus it did not surprise me at all, as I waited for Judy in Ratso's apartment that evening, to see Ratso himself waltz in dressed either as a Russian Cossack dancer or a gay matador, and in the mood I was in I didn't particularly care to learn which. I tapped my fingertips impatiently upon the plaster head of Ratso's life-size statue of the Virgin Mary and waited for my host to reveal the point-of-purchase details of his new mix-and-match outfit. Yet Ratso always ceased to amaze me. He said not a word about his outlandish wardrobe. Instead, his entire focus appeared to involve a small wicker basket he was carrying in his right hand.

"Kinkstah!" he shouted. "You'll never believe where I've been."

"At an Easter-egg hunt in a mental hospital," I said.

"No," said Ratso. "At a flea market on Canal Street."

"That's wonderful, Ratso. Where's Judy?"

"Don't worry. She's coming."

"Sexually?"

"No, that was last night. Remember, I was a witness to the actual climax itself. *'Tim! Tim! Oh, Tim, your prick is bigger than Kinky's! I'm just using Kinky to get to Ratso!'* "

"Seriously, Rat. Who do you think Tim is?"

"How the hell do I know who Tim is? Judy's a hot young chick from North Carolina. She's hosing you after knowing you just one day. With that kind of sketchy, yet disturbing and rather limited background data, my current hypothesis is that

Tim's her brother. That'll be fifty-seven dollars. I'll throw in room and board."

"Mother of God, Ratso! You *would* make a good California pop psychologist! You're already dressed for the part, you've got a degree in psychology. Of course, your bedside manner's kind of weak—"

"I've got my *master's* in psychology. From the University of Wisconsin."

"Why didn't you get your Ph.D.?"

"A spider bit me on the scrotum."

"I'm sorry to hear that."

"Actually, I didn't get a Ph.D. because it wasn't really what I wanted."

"You mean Wisconsin didn't offer a program in Jesus, Hitler, and Bob Dylan? I'm surprised."

"Okay, so you don't agree with my analysis. Who do *you* think Tim is? Timothy Leary?"

"That's always possible. Tiny Tim's another potential candidate. They're both fine Americans. The Jewboys co-billed with Leary one memorable night in Columbus, Ohio. My old friend from the Peace Corps, John Morgan, was there. He said the show 'flowed well both inside and outside of Leary's brain.' Just about everybody there was cookin' on another planet except Morgan and myself and sometimes I've wondered about Morgan. As far as Tiny goes, he's a 'serious soul nobody takes seriously,' to quote Billy Joe Shaver, who, by the way, was not on the bill at Columbus, Ohio. I've performed with Tiny several times in New York."

"A fascinating itinerary. But the question is, which Tim performed with Judy?"

"These are early days, Ratso, but I have read my Sherlock Holmes—"

"Probably on this very couch when you weren't busy hosing—"

"—and I have formed my own methods—strictly as a hobby, you understand—of deductive reasoning. These are very much my own ideas, but, like an undescended testicle, everything, of course, derives from Holmesian dogma. In the beginning there was Holmes."

"Just remember the sign somebody put in front of the Catholic church: BEWARE OF DOGMA."

"Yes, yes, my dear Watson. But my trained eye may have caught a small detail you may have missed, thereby establishing a more likely scenario than your incestuous-brother theory. Did you notice the small ornament on the delicate silver chain dangling upon her breast?"

"I did notice she had big tits. I didn't notice the small ornament dangling between them because your head was also dangling there."

"Very well, Watson. Then you could not observe that the object in question hanging on the chain was a small silver airplane!"

"A small silver airplane! Sherlock! What a brilliant discovery! Now tell me what you make of the contents of this ordinary-looking wicker basket?"

"What're you trying to do? Derail my chain of deductive reasoning? What *are* these macabre, satanic little things? Doll heads?"

"Not doll heads. They're little Negro *puppet heads* and for four bucks today on Canal Street I bought all two dozen of them. What a great fucking deal!"

"Cornered the market, did you?"

"Well, you never know, Kinkstah!"

"I know one thing. If I had the authority to sign a document that would place you in a mental hospital for the rest of your life, I'd sign it right now for your own safety and protection."

"Could I take the puppet heads with me?"

"Sure. Waltz in there with the puppet heads and the polar-bear head and you'd never come out."

"Sherlock! I just realized the significance of Judy's little silver airplane!"

"Good work, Watson. Pray tell us your theory."

"The brother in North Carolina was hosing her, then he ran off and became a drummer for the Jefferson Airplane."

"Ah, my dear Watson, you bring a charming naïveté to our little puzzle. But this is a far more wicked world, Watson, than you may envision. And I believe we shall find the true significance of the little silver airplane to be far more sinister."

At this point in the conversation, an incredibly loud buzzing sound filled the little apartment.

"Hell," said Ratso disgustedly, "there's always someone at the door just when I have to launch a growler."

"Ah, Watson, you bring such color and humanity to our little problem. But if I'm not mistaken, the lady herself will soon be here and she may lay the matter to rest."

"That's great, Sherlock. She'll lay the matter. You'll lay the lady. And I'll lay some cable."

"Alimentary canal, my dear Watson, alimentary canal."

8

The Monkey's Paw was not the kind of place you'd choose if you wanted to impress a young lady you'd recently met. On the other paw, if your last theater of operations had been Ratso's apartment, almost any place you went would seem like a step up in the world. To get into the Monkey's Paw, of course, quite literally, you had to step down. The joint was one floor below street level and you could watch people's feet as they walked by on the sidewalk, giving the place all the ambience of a basement apartment. If the scene depressed you, you knew you couldn't kill yourself by jumping out the window. The only way to take a Brodie in the Monkey's Paw was to drink yourself to death. Many of its patrons did precisely that.

"Nice place," said Judy, as about eight guys at the bar ogled her lasciviously. "You really pull out all the stops to impress a girl."

"Give it a chance," I said. "I've only been here a few times, but the place does seem to grow on you. Besides, they provide weasel-dust in the dumper."

"Sounds charming," she said, sounding fresh out of charm herself.

Judy might've bolted at that moment had not a very large man with a very large head suddenly filled the doorway. I took Judy by the arm and guided her to a little cranny between the bar and a window with a view of people's feet walking by on Christopher Street. It was becoming obvious even to my untrained, rather cavalier eye, that, given half the chance, Judy would've been attached to one of those pairs of feet and walked right out of the place and my life. I did what I could to put her at ease.

"Now don't get your feathers ruffled," I said. "You and I just got to know each other a little bit before we got to know each other. What're you drinking?"

"Diet hemlock," she said.

I ordered a couple of Jameson Irish Whiskeys and two pints of Guinness so they wouldn't get lonely. If I didn't pour a few drinks down Judy's neck pretty soon she was bound to bug out for the dugout and then I would be lonely. That was all right, I figured. I could live with lonely.

Usually, after two people conduct sexual intercourse, certain social barriers are removed and they feel more comfortable together. Possibly because our recent little hose-a-thon had attracted a small spectator element, or possibly because Judy had invoked Tim's name instead of mine at the critical moment, she'd been deeply mortified and had repressed the whole incident, thereby accounting for the chill that seemed to exist between the two of us. It didn't appear as if she'd be unbosoming herself of any pertinent information about Tim any time soon. Indeed, at the moment, even small talk was hard to come by, so to speak.

Just about the time the drinks arrived in our dark little corner of the Monkey's Paw, so did the big man with the big head and two of his drinking buddies. Big Head had a very loud laugh for such small quarters and he wasn't afraid to use it. A tall, thin, blond fellow stood behind us playing hide-and-seek by humorously sticking his head inside the window curtain every time we looked around. He was wearing white pants and had one hand in his pocket.

"Watch this," he said, as he repeatedly flicked a Bic lighter inside his pocket dangerously close to his scrotum.

"That's a pretty good trick you've got going for yourself," I said.

"Learned it in Korea," he said, briefly taking his head out from behind the curtain.

"Don't mind Ted," said Big Head. "He doesn't bite."

"Nothing by mouth," said Ted.

"Have a cigar," said the third guy, in a thick British accent. "It's a girl."

"It certainly is," said Big Head, looking at Judy.

"Nothing by mouth," said Ted.

"My name's Peter Myers," said the Brit, as he handed me the cigar. "Ignore these two blokes. They've had too many gorilla biscuits."

"What's a gorilla biscuit?" asked Judy.

"It's what you take when you've taken too much weasel-dust," said Myers.

"What's weasel-dust?" asked Judy. She was turning into quite a little conversationalist.

"Nothing by mouth," said Ted.

Shortly thereafter, the guy called Ted and the guy with the big head went into the dumper together and never came back. Myers told us about his plan to open a British gourmet food shop in the Village. He planned to call it "Myers of Keswick," he said. Then Myers disappeared into the dumper and he didn't come back either.

I ordered another round of Jameson's. I was starting to like Jameson's. I was even starting to like Judy. She was beginning to look mildly enticing just sitting there drinking and thinking. There was something slightly enigmatic and appealing about her background. Her foreground wasn't bad either.

"Who *were* those guys?" I asked the bartender when he brought the drinks.

"Just general troublemakers," he said. "Pete Myers has been talking about opening up that shop for years. Most ridiculous idea I ever heard. You think there's any great craving for British gourmet cooking in New York? Now we serve shepherd's pie, but that's about as far as it goes. Whole idea's a pipe dream. Never happen."

"What about the tall, thin guy who was flicking his Bic inside his trousers' pocket?"

"I'd stay away from him, too. He's a Canadian whose main pleasure in life seems to be irritating Americans. His name's Ted Mann. He writes for *National Lampoon*."

"He *was* kind of funny," said Judy.

"A little bit of Ted Mann goes a long way," said the bartender with a grim expression.

"What about the big guy with the big head and loud laugh?" I asked. "Who's he?"

"That one you *really* don't want to know. He's a reporter for the *Daily News* and he can be one of the worst-behaved animals I've seen. An Irishman. Makes Ted Mann look like a choirboy."

"He seemed nice to me," said Judy.

"Don't get too attached," said the bartender ominously. "He's about to get eighty-sixed from the Monkey's Paw."

"A fate worse than death," I said, glancing around at the smoke-laden crowd of drunken, depressed-looking denizens at the bar. "What's his name?"

"Mike McGovern," said the bartender.

Possibly in an unconscious act of empathy with the about-to-be-eighty-sixed Irishman, I ordered two more shots of Jameson Irish Whiskey and another round of Guinness. Maybe it was just the alcohol or maybe it was the dim lighting in the dank little place, but Judy was loosening up a bit and now was starting to appear quite ravishing. With her red hair flowing around her shoulders and her brown eyes finally beginning to smile a bit, she looked nothing less than an Irish beauty.

"Are you Irish?" I asked.

"Of course. Are you going to smoke that cigar?"

"I'll probably get around to it one of these days."

"Then take it out of your mouth." I obeyed. "Now kiss me," she said.

Our lips came together and stayed that way very probably a little longer than either of us had intended. It was a soft, sensuous, clinging, slightly salty kiss. A kiss of life in a city of death.

"Now that we know who everyone else is," I said, "why don't you tell me about Tim."

9

As the deep brown river of Guinness continued to flow that night, along with the occasional tributary of Jameson's, a stream of memories began to flow as well, emanating from Judy's heart and my own until it mingled at last with the deeper, darker waters in the muddy, winding river of life. As the stream of memory flowed slowly to the sea, I found myself urinating an uncanny number of times in the dank, dismal dumper of the Monkey's Paw. Upon each urinary trip I searched for the spoor of Myers, McGovern, or Ted Mann, but this unholy trinity appeared to have vanished into whatever thin air there existed within the crowded, congested confines of the Monkey's Paw. On a goodly number of my dumper trips, however, I did notice the same individual, a small, wiry, twitching creature, dispensing tiny tinfoil packets to patrons of the Paw. The merchant of the men's room, of course, was known as the Weasel. The product he disseminated was known as weasel-dust. I had never tried any and I wasn't sure that I wanted to. I didn't want to disappear like McGovern, Myers, and Ted Mann.

"One of the hardest things in life is to be so far away from someone you're so close to," Judy was saying in the near-drunken tones that are always the truth. "The last time I made love to a man before last night was five years ago. It was the night before Tim left for Vietnam."

"Long time between dreams," I said.

"Oh no. Tim and I have never been between dreams. We're always in each other's hearts. That's why I wear his little silver plane."

She twisted the silver chain around her finger and made the tiny aircraft perform a few neat barrel-rolls through the beautiful, slightly moist, valley between her breasts. If there was a tiny little pilot aboard he was getting one hell of a view.

"Tim and I were high school sweethearts—"

"I was in the gay men's choir—"

"I think in a way we still are high school sweethearts," she said, ignoring me and everyone else in the room. "It's sort of a Romeo-and-Juliet type of thing. Our families never approved. He was my first love and I'm sure he'll be my last. It's always been that way. Tim and me against the world."

"I like the odds."

Maybe I'd had a few too many drinks, but from the way she was talking I was having a hard time figuring out how I fit into the picture. Indeed, I was beginning to wonder if the little love-in on Ratso's couch the night before had actually happened. It was a good thing I had witnesses, I thought.

"It was probably just the Peruvian marching powder talking last night," I said. "I really shouldn't consider you my official CPA."

"What's a CPA ?" she said half-guardedly. The other half, I noticed, didn't seem to really give a damn.

"Current pelvic affiliation," I said. Judy did not even smile.

"That's really reaching," she said, her face an emotionless porcelain mask. "Like all those people reaching for the last helicopter at the end of the war."

Math was never my long suit, and at the moment I was so high I needed a stepladder to scratch my ass, but, by visualizing a large abacus, I was able to do some basic sums in my head. Tim had left for Vietnam as a Navy pilot about five years ago. The war had ended roughly three years ago. That didn't leave Tim a lot of flying time. I wanted to ask "Where's Tim now?" or "What happened to Tim?" but I didn't. I just lit the cigar, took a few puffs, and waited. It was just as well.

"Tim was shot down during one of Nixon's Christmas bombings. The plane crashed in a rice paddy and he was listed as missing in action for over two years. Six months ago they recovered the plane and identified his body and sent him home to North Carolina. He was buried with full military honors. His parents wouldn't speak to me at the funeral. It was like they were almost blaming me for his death. I left for New York the same day. Now here I am, drunk at the Monkey's Paw."

"You could do worse."

"What could be worse than the Monkey's Paw?"

"The men's room of the Monkey's Paw."

"You know, it's funny," Judy said, fondling the little plane again and staring into a sky that wasn't there, "but over the past six months I've also felt like blaming myself for Tim's death."

"That's quite natural," I said, "but totally unfounded. Assessing the blame should always be left to God and small children. You didn't start the war. You weren't responsible for the devastation over there or the ongoing nightmare that's resulted over here. The war started in Beverly Hills in a delicatessen called Nate and Al's. It began at table number seven with an argument between Jackie Mason and Marty Allen over how to properly prepare and pronounce the words: 'kreplach soup.' John Wayne and Jane Fonda happened to be in the place at the time and they, of course, took sides and from there things just got out of hand."

"But I let him go," she said.

"You've got to let 'em go. Give 'em wings and let 'em fly. Sometimes they come back to you. Sometimes they don't."

"Sometimes they come back to you in a bag."

I put one arm around Judy and held her tightly against me there at the bar. One little tear fell from one brown eye for one poor sucker who fell from a faraway sky only days before everybody else came home. Anything you do is cold comfort for a loss like that. No matter how hard you try, a living soul is not something you can ever shelter and make safe from sorrow. All you can do is hug the girl on the barstool next to you in the Monkey's Paw. All you can do is put your other arm around her and try to hold her. But she was spoken for forever. She wouldn't be held. It was like reaching for a helicopter you knew you were never going to make.

10

I hailed a passing hack on Seventh Avenue and got Judy inside it and we waved good-bye to each other as the cabby shot off through the traffic like a bottle rocket. I wasn't in a hurry myself, so I thought I'd walk around the Village for a while. When you don't have a home, I figured, it's just as easy to walk as it is to take a taxi. But a home wasn't the only thing I didn't have. I didn't have much of a career to speak of either. Just a relentless series of Sunday-night gigs at the Lone Star Cafe that almost paid for the Peruvian marching powder. The only reason I wasn't walking around like a spinning ghost, totally monstered on weasel-dust, was that I didn't know the Weasel's name and he didn't look like the kind of guy who'd give you free samples. Aside from no home and no career, the other thing I had was no money. On top of all this, after having talked with Judy for half the night in the Paw, it appeared highly doubtful that I possessed a current pelvic affiliation.

All in all I felt considerably Christ-like as I cruised down

Christopher Street, my cowboy drag drawing more than the usual number of stares from patrons of a leather bar just across the way. Like Jesus, I was without a home, without a wife, without a job. Also like Jesus, I was a skinny Jew who traveled around the countryside irritating people. It was good work if you could get it.

As the night grew colder and the streets grew darker, my thoughts turned colder and darker as well. There were lots of Tims up there somewhere, I figured, who'd inadvertently stepped on a precocious rainbow and gone to Jesus long before their time. There were lots of Judys out there somewhere also who'd been sentenced to live a long, laborious, loveless half-life in this wretched, war-weary world. If the truth be told, I was a Judy who longed to be a Tim. I had lost someone, too, quite recently. She was the prettiest girl in the world with a flower in her hair. She'd kissed a windshield at ninety-five miles per hour in her Ferrari and went directly to "the Jesus of her choosin'" without passing through my life again and without collecting two hundred zillion dollars. She was a poor little rich girl from Vancouver. She was only twenty-seven. I'd been far away at the time of her death, but I'd blamed myself the same way Judy blamed herself for the loss of her young airman. Judy had her little silver airplane. I had my little snapshot of Kacey as a child holding the hand of her father, Jake the Snake. The photo was taken at a little airport somewhere in Canada. The small planes on the runway and the cars in the parking lot and the clothes they were wearing and the carefree smiles on their faces all looked like vintage 1950s. Everything else about the picture looked like a quarter ever after midnight in the sky. Sure, I'll get over Kacey. That'll be the day, all right. The day Judy gets over Tim. The day they tear down the Berlin Wall. The day the New York Rangers win the Stanley Cup. Sooner or later you had to face it. Some things you never really get over. The most you can truly hope for is to some day get above that little airport.

"You goddamn bastard!" shouted a voice behind me. "What the hell do you think you're doin'?"

I turned from my reverie just in time to see a clean-cut, extremely well-muscled young man rushing directly toward me like a human steam engine. At the last moment, he swerved to confront a rather rotund young beat cop busily writing out a parking ticket.

"What do you think I'm doin'," said the cop. "I'm writing you a parking ticket, you fucking punk."

"It's fucking one o'clock in the morning!"

"That's still a fucking fire hydrant!"

A small crowd of degenerates had by now gathered on the sidewalk, some obviously dazed on drugs. Several others, it seemed, were merely wandering around in some form of homosexual fugue. Apparently, this kind of small-time altercation was better than no action at all. I had to admit I blended in with the crowd a little better than I would've liked. The two warring parties, suddenly aware of their audience, began to polish their invective.

"Look at that shiny leather belt," said the young man. "You must've just gotten out of the academy."

"Just in time to write you a ticket," said the cop, making a show of checking the license number.

"Look, uh—Cooperman. That your name? Cooperman?"

"That's it, pal," said the cop with a malicious grin. "That's the name I'm writin' on your ticket."

"Cooperman, look, you're a fuckin' rookie. You've got to learn to let the small shit slide or you'll never make detective. You'll spend the next twenty years walking around putting tickets on parked cars."

"I'm off to a good start then," said Cooperman, handing the guy the ticket and winking broadly to the crowd. "Here's yours, pal."

As the crowd drifted away the young man stood on the curb studying the ticket. Something indefinable drew me toward him.

"Tough luck," I said. "Things almost got a little heated there."

"He was a fat man walking a thin line," said the guy. "But that was nothing. In New York that's a friendly conversation with a cop."

I introduced myself and invited him to drop by the Lone Star some Sunday night. He said he'd try. He said his name was Rambam. Steve Rambam. Said he was a rabbinical student.

"How do you spell that name?" I asked.

"Any way you like," he said.

"It's a funny name," I said.

"So's Kinky," said Rambam. "With that big black hat I knew you had to be a cowboy or a fagola. You *are* a cowboy, aren't you?"

"Yup," I said. "Been ridin' 'cross the desert on a horse with no legs. Good luck, Rambam."

Rambam patted the rear of the car. He was smiling as he walked around to open the door.

"I've already had good luck," he said. "That fucking cop didn't check my trunk."

"What's in the trunk?"

"A dead Nazi."

11

"Okay, Sherlock," said Ratso the following afternoon, "your suspicions about Judy were correct and mine were—"

"Totally ludicrous."

"Well, let's just say 'not borne out by the facts.' But I have to admit your demonstration of deductive reasoning, what with the little airplane, the war recently over, the intense climax, the shouting of the wrong name—"

"It wasn't the wrong name. It just wasn't *my* name."

"Well, normally you shout the name of the person you're hosing."

"Normally you're not staring up at a polar bear's head with guys like you and Tom Baker heckling the performance."

"What I'm trying to tell you is if you ever grow up you've got the makings of a pretty good amateur detective, Sherlock."

"Well, thanks, Ratso."

"Just don't give up your day job."

"I don't have a day job."

"Sorry. I forgot. Well, anyway, you'd make a good private dick, Kinkstah."

"There's nothing private about anybody's dick in this apartment. I've really got to find my own place to live."

"You never heard Phil Ochs or Michael Bloomfield complain about staying here."

"That's because they're dead, Ratso."

"Don't blame the fucking couch."

"I'm not blaming the fucking couch. I'm blaming the fucking world. And most of all, I'm blaming you for getting me involved in this fucking ridiculous conversation."

For a few moments a sullen silence prevailed in the congested little apartment. Then, like a rather sick couple making up, Ratso and I decided to walk down to Chinatown together for lunch.

"Big Wong's, Kinkstah!" Ratso shouted. "Roast pork!" Ratso always pronounced the word "pork" as "pawk" and this never failed to irritate me slightly, but under the circumstances, I let it slide. Good Chinese food has kept the Jewish people together for thousands of years.

It is not precisely clear which of the two of us first discovered Big Wong's at 67 Mott Street. All that is certain is that Ratso and I have dexterously manipulated enough chopsticks there to have, by this time, crocheted a large quilt which was, unfortunately, about the only thing that might've kept us warm as we legged it up Canal Street toward Chinatown.

"Jesus," said Ratso, rubbing his hands together like an insect, "what do all the bums and the poor people do when it gets this cold?"

"Don't ask me," I said. "I live on your couch."

We hooked a right on Mott and soon were inside the warm, friendly confines of Big Wong's. The waiters and busboys all chanted their ritual greeting upon our arrival: "Ooooh-laah-laah! Oooh-laah-laah! Kee-Kee! Chee-Chee!" The latter obviously were terms of endearment for myself and Ratso.

"I'm serious, Kinkstah!" said Ratso when we'd been seated. "You've got a very convoluted mind. You ought to consider becoming some kind of detective."

"First I'd need something to detect."

"Why not start by finding the menu," said Ratso. "I don't see any on the table."

We ordered an enormous amount of food, the whole megillah ending with Ratso insisting upon his usual double order of roast pork over scrambled eggs.

"No roast pawk!" said the waiter.

"No roast pawk!" shouted Ratso, becoming highly agitato.

"No roast pawk!" affirmed the waiter.

"That's what happens," I said to Ratso, "when you have breakfast at four o'clock."

Roast pork, I'd observed in the past, was so killer bee at Big Wong's that it often ran out before anything else on the menu. The other moderately interesting thing I observed was that the waiter's Chinese pronunciation of the word "pork" and Ratso's New York version of the word were precisely identical. It was a small couch after all.

"No roast pork," Ratso muttered, after the waiter had left. "I just can't believe it."

"Pinch yourself," I said.

Afterward, with Ratso belching like an Eskimo in traditional appreciation of the meal, we walked up Mott to Canal, hooked a left one block, and ankled it up colorful Mulberry Street in Little Italy. We stopped at Louie and Johnny's little shop right next to Luna's Restaurant. Amongst other decorative items for sale, there was a large bust of Elvis in the front window.

"I didn't realize Elvis was Italian," I said, as we loitered on the sidewalk.

"He wasn't," said Ratso. "He was Jewish on his mother's side, which was good enough for Hitler and good enough for me."

"Okay. If he was Jewish, where was he bar-mitzvahed, who was the rabbi, and who was the caterer?"

"You think I'm kidding? His mother's family kept their Jewishness a secret, which was not uncommon in the Deep South—"

"As well as a few other places—"

"—because nobody could pronounce the word 'schmuck' in Biloxi."

"Cultural deprivation."

"But his brother's name was Aaron, there's a Star of David on both of their tombstones, and both sons were always very close to their mother."

"That clinches it," I said. "Not to mention the undeniable fact that when compared side-by-side, Elvis's famous, smoldering, sparking black eyes bear an almost uncanny resemblance to those of Anne Frank."

"They *do* look like Anne Frank's. I've never noticed that, Kinkstah."

"That's why God punished you by taking away the thing you love most—roast pork."

"It's possible," said Ratso, as we entered the shop.

"Hey, Gene Autry!" shouted Louie from behind the cluttered counter. "Where's your horse?"

"He's out back hosing Trigger," I said. "He's a homosexual horse."

"He came to the right town," said Johnny.

Even though Tom Baker had made it his life's work to bust my chops for buying "esoteric off-brands" of cigarettes, I nonetheless bought a pack of Players and a few cigars.

"Those cigarettes'll kill you," said Ratso.

"That's all right," said Louie. "Those cigars'll kill everybody else."

"Works for me," I said.

Moments later, walking down Mulberry Street, I lit up one of the cigars and Ratso wasted no time in bumming the other one from me. So we walked along together, puffing cigars, oblivious to any cares in the world, watching the smoke spiral lazily into the narrow New York sky, accompanied, of course, by measure after measure of tinny, eternal Italian street music. Little did I think at the time that Ratso's half-humorous suggestion that I become a detective might soon be a reality. Little did I realize that even then a cold, sinister mind was methodically at work, and far more swiftly than cigarettes and cigars, it was ruthlessly determined to destroy me and everybody else.

12

"This is strange," said Ratso later that evening as we returned to the apartment.

"What's strange?" I said. "Did you catch Mahatma Gandhi cleaning your bathroom?"

"There's three messages on the answering machine."

"That *is* strange. I didn't know you had three friends."

"One's from George Metesky. One's from Jimmy Carter. And one's from somebody named Barry Freed."

"Who's Jimmy Carter?"

"This is serious, Kinkstah. A different name each time, but it's the same voice on all the messages. It's a deep, gruff, raspy voice, but it sounds kind of familiar."

"Maybe it's Tom Waits."

"Maybe it's the perfect opportunity for you to sharpen up on your sleuthing. Listen while I play them back."

I puffed on the soggy dog turd that was all that was left of my cigar and listened to Ratso's answering machine. I had to admit that even though the caller was obviously trying to disguise his voice, it sounded kind of familiar to me, too. I also had to admit it was kind of fun playing modern-day Sherlock Holmes to Ratso's colorful, sometimes tedious, but always kindhearted Dr. Watson. Quite a team we made, all right. Now all we needed was a game for the team to play. And if I didn't miss my guess, the game was afoot.

"Play it again, Sam," I said, growing more interested. Ratso played the messages again.

"I tell you, Sherlock, there's something familiar about that voice. I know I've heard it before."

"Of course you have, Watson. We've played the tape three times now."

"Before that," Ratso said irritably.

"Now, cast your mind back, Watson. President Carter is probably not in the habit of calling here often. Do the other two names mean anything to you?"

"I never heard of that last one. Barry Freed. But George Metesky. I know who that is."

"How would you like to share it with the rest of the class?"

"I've talked to Metesky a few times. The voice wasn't his."

"Yes, my dear Watson. But who *is* Metesky?"

"George Metesky was known as 'The Mad Bomber of New York.' He used to work for Con Ed in the fifties and when they fired him he began bombing various Con Ed facilities around the city and generally scaring the shit out of everybody. He was caught finally and sent to prison but released several years ago. He now lives with his mother in Connecticut."

"You *know* this guy?"

"Yeah. He was kind of a character. Never really hurt anybody. He was sort of a folk hero to the underground and the Yippies and people like that. Should I invite him over?"

"Looks like he's already been here. But it's curious that the caller doesn't use either of our names, yet several times refers to us as 'you guys.' How does he know that I'm crashing with you?"

"Maybe he's spying on us."

"Let's apply a little deductive reasoning. The mysterious caller is someone who knows where you live, knows I'm staying with you, knows about George Metesky, and is sort of a prankster at heart. His voice is familiar-sounding even when disguised, because, though neither of us has seen him in a long time, we both know him. I suspect the last name he gave, Barry Freed, is the pseudonym under which he's currently operating—"

"Abbie Hoffman!"

"But of course, my dear Watson. Now all we have to do is sit tight for a while and if I'm not very much mistaken, our long-lost old friend from the underground should be surfacing soon right here on Prince Street."

"But he hasn't been in touch with anybody in over a year and rumor has it that the feds are really turning up the heat in order to catch him."

"Another good reason for me to move out of here."

"It's a pretty good reason for *me* to move out of here. What do we do, Sherlock?"

"We wait for Barry Freed. And now, Watson, if you'll kindly hand me down my syringe from the mantel."

13

Dear Abbie, I thought, as I puffed a Players cigarette, where are you tonight? Indeed, it appeared as if we were about to find out. I reflected briefly about the first time I'd met Abbie. It was at the Chelsea Hotel, room 1010—Janis Joplin's old room. It had been about five years ago, sometime during the winter of '74, just before Abbie had gone underground and become a fugitive from the government of the United States of America. Abbie had invited me to come to New York from Texas to be the co-bill on a farewell show for him at the Village Gate. I didn't know, of course, that it would be a farewell show. I also didn't know that the other half of the bill would be a videotape of Abbie's recent vasectomy operation. Nevertheless, the show had gone smoothly, with none of the usual bickering between the performers over who would have top billing.

He'd looked like a hunted, haunted man even then, that first night at the Chelsea, his dark eyes shining everywhere like a troubled, visionary clown. In the next five years he would hide out with me on at least three extended occasions, first at our ranch in Texas, then at my apartment in Malibu, and finally, at my place on King Street in Chappaqua, New York. Where he'd stayed the rest of the time he was underground was anybody's guess. The fact that the search for him had apparently intensified, coupled with my strong suspicion that he was already in the city and would soon be paying a visit to Ratso and myself, did not bode well for Abbie, I felt. Even when he'd stayed with me he'd been tired of running. Maybe he was finally reaching the end of his revolutionary rope.

"Kinkela," Abbie had said that night at the Chelsea, "I'm glad you came up for the show. But promise me you'll close the set with 'Ride 'em Jewboy.'"

"I don't know," I'd told him. "That's kind of a mournful, funereal song about the Holocaust and the diaspora and it ain't exactly going to leave 'em laughing. I don't think it's the right song to end with."

"It's not the right song," he'd said. "It's the perfect song."

Abbie had been set up on a fraudulent drug charge by government agents who wanted him for other reasons, one of which was not taking life on this planet as seriously as they thought he should. When I'd done the show for him in New York he was out on bail. By the time the last chords of "Ride 'em Jewboy" had disappeared into the night, so had Abbie.

My reflections were suddenly shattered by what seemed to be the buzzing of a gigantic, radioactive bee, which I soon realized was merely the incredibly loud buzzing of Ratso's intercom system.

"It would appear that we have a visitor, Watson," I said, getting up from the couch.

"What if they're monitoring his calls?" said Ratso in a sudden wave of anxiety. "What if they know he's coming here and they catch him with us?"

"Ratso, have you ever read the book *Prison Rape as a Positive Experience?*"

The buzzer sounded again, loud, long, and menacing. Ratso stood by the intercom, as motionless and pallid as a plaster Virgin Mary.

"Either push the button and ask who's there," I said, "or I'll have to go out and get a very large flyswatter and stop this buzzing."

Ratso pushed the button.

"Who's there?" he whispered furtively.

"FBI!" shouted a voice. "OPEN UP!"

14

Ratso leaped sideways from the intercom almost as if someone had asked him would he please pay the check. I had to admit that I was a bit startled myself. Nonetheless, I recovered my composure in time to cajole a very shaken Ratso into pushing the button again and once more requesting the identity of our mysterious visitor.

"Who's there?" Ratso asked more forcefully.

Abbie Hoffman's unique cackle came clearly through the intercom. He was a brilliant, gentle, colorful character, and of all his many talents, his innate ability to fully live the comedy of life may have been his long suit. He'd been on the run for five years and still he was the eternal joker in the deck. Even though he'd known all along that the deck was stacked against him.

"Who's there?" Ratso demanded again.

"Barry Freed," said Abbie. "Let me in or I'll corrupt all your young people, fuck all your daughters, and create anarchy in your streets."

"Better let him in," I said.

Ratso took a deep breath and pushed the button that unlocked the door to the building. We listened to the soft buzzing sound followed by the sound of a door opening. There's lots of doors swinging open and closed in this world, I thought. And there're lots of people in our lives leaving and entering doors that we cannot see. All we can hope is that when the Lord closes the door, He opens a little window.

We waited.

Before long we heard the elevator doors opening, steps in the hallway, the strange, nocturnal, ravenlike tapping at our chamber door. Then Ratso began the always laborious process of unlocking and unchaining and unbolting the door to his apartment of personal treasures containing nothing anyone else in the world would've ever conceivably coveted. Then Abbie Hoffman came in from the cold.

"Jesus Christ," he said, "this is the funkiest crash pad I've seen since the Summer of Love."

"The maid passed away," I said.

"Rat! Kinkela!" said Abbie, hugging us both in turn. "I've missed you guys. You never call. You never write."

"We might've," said Ratso, "if we'd ever known where the hell you were."

"Half the time *I* didn't know where the fuck I was. Every time I thought I was safe, I'd suddenly find the long arm of the law reaching out to grab me by the balls. It's a deadly game of hide-and-seek and it only ends when they find you or you turn yourself in, which I'm never going to do."

"You can't run forever, Abbie," said Ratso, taking Abbie's coat and steering him gently toward the couch.

Abbie looked weary like an old man, fragile like a child. He was bloodied but unbowed, ragged but right. He had kind of a Lenny Bruce–Joe Hill–Tom Joad spirit about him. Like Jesus Christ, I thought whimsically, he's true to his school, a martyr in the making, if I ever saw one, a martyr to the sixties he believed in.

"Abbie's not here," said Abbie. "The same guys that got Dillinger and Bonnie and Clyde and Pretty Boy Floyd got Abbie. Abbie's dead."

"Then he probably wouldn't want the remaining half of this pastrami sandwich," said Ratso, opting to leaven the proceedings.

"Abbie wouldn't," he said. "But Barry Freed's fucking starving. That's who I am now. Barry Freed. I live in upstate New York, and, believe it or not, I've gotten very involved in the environmental movement. I'm trying to save the St. Lawrence River."

"First, Barry," I said, "you'd better try to save yourself."

"That's not going to be easy," he said. "I think somebody followed me here."

"What!" said Ratso, almost dropping the pastrami sandwich.

The man who called himself Barry Freed crept over to the window in a low crouch, signaling Ratso and myself to stay where we were. Using the Virgin Mary for cover, he rose slowly, almost sinuously against her unprotesting plaster body, to peer fatefully down at the street.

"There he is," he said. "The same guy who was following me earlier. Stay away from the windows."

"What's he look like?" said Ratso nervously.

"Tall guy. Long blond hair. Wearing an old army jacket."

"What's he doing now?" asked Ratso.

"Standing in front of the bakery across the street," said Abbie, peeping cautiously over the windowsill, "and pretending to eat a bagel. He's looking up at this building."

"Fucking great," said Ratso.

I didn't know if Abbie's perceptions of the man he saw on the street were accurate, paranoid, or even delusional. The only way to find out was to look for myself. So I began creeping up along the closest line from the skid marks to the Virgin Mary. Abbie was still staring intently into the street, crouching low, half-hiding like a ragged pilgrim behind the Mother of God.

"Abbie," I said.

"Barry," he hissed. "And stay down. I don't want you guys dragged into this with me."

"It's a little late for that, Barry. You come back and rest on the couch for a while. Let me take a turn at the watchtower."

Abbie backtracked slowly, then, muttering like a small child, went obediently over to the couch and lay down, betraying himself only with a middle-aged Jewish sigh. I took up his former position and gazed down into the street. There was absolutely no one standing in front of the bakery across the street. There was no one anywhere on the street even vaguely resembling the guy Abbie had described.

"What the hell am I going to do?" said Abbie. "Now I can't leave here."

Under the circumstances of course, it probably wouldn't be big fun for anybody to leave at the moment. Not to mention the cold, undeniable fact that, as so often happens in life, there was nowhere else to go.

Abbie stared at me helplessly. Ratso stared at me helplessly. The polar bear stared at me helplessly. The Virgin Mary stared at me helplessly.

"Try pretending to eat a pastrami sandwich," I said.

15

In Hawaii, a slow-paced, beautiful land of mostly brown-skinned people, there are only white pigeons. In New York, a hectic, hell-bent land of mostly white people, there are almost exclusively dark-colored pigeons. At this writing, it is not clear whether this little celebrated, seldom researched phenomenon evolved naturally over the years or whether it is merely a puerile prank played upon the peoples of the earth by the Baby Jesus, possibly as a very early science project.

Was anyone really watching Abbie Hoffman? A better question might have been, Was anyone really watching any of us? There were, in fact, only two occasions in my entire life when I could be sure someone was, indeed, watching my every move. Both, for whatever it was worth, involved Tom Baker.

The first instance when I knew someone was watching had occurred some years ago in Hollywood when I was going with a girl named Twink, hanging out with the Bakerman and our brilliant, crazy friend Fox Harris, and driving a 1948

Hudson in the fast lane. At the time I was sporting a Hebrew natural-style haircut that made me look and often feel like Angela Davis. The only time I was particularly touchy about my moss was when I woke up from a power nap and the shape of my head had flattened on both sides so that it resembled more than anything else a rocket ship with a payload of pubic hair. Because of this migrant moss situation, until I could get to a hairbrush and a mirror, I was understandably somewhat grumpy upon awakening. The Bakerman, always a master at busting other people's chops, took advantage of my vulnerable nature when I made the mistake of crashing on his davenport one balmy afternoon in L.A. I'd had, apparently, a rather unnerving, mildly homosexual dream and thus, upon awakening with my eyelids sealed shut and various by-products of cocaine dripping into my Reform Jewish sinuses, I was a bit more grumpy than usual. I definitely did not wish to see or be seen by man, woman, child, or beast until I had my moss situation properly sorted out.

As I flung my orbs open to the dying California afternoon, I observed a fairly sizable live audience—thirty or forty people—though it seemed like more in five neat rows of folding chairs like a theater-in-the-round, all of whom had apparently been watching me sleep, watching me dream, and now were intently watching my hair. Baker, who looked a lot like the swashbuckling Billy Bigelow in *Carousel,* was nervously busy serving drinks, making coffee, keeping the customers satisfied. I got up in a very surly mood and stumbled, to light applause, across to the dumper where I threw some cold water on my face and straightened out my moss. By the time I returned, Baker was shaking hands and saying farewells to the last of the crowd like a proud father at a bar-mitzvah reception. Then he went over to his old linoleum drainboard and poured us both a hefty shot of tequila.

"Where the hell'd you find a matinee crowd like that?" I said.

"You haven't lost it, Pinky—I mean Stinky, I mean Finky, I mean Dinky, I mean Slinky—oh, right, I mean *Kinky,*" he chanted, handing me a jigger. "You can still draw a crowd. Of course, you can also clear a room with the best of 'em. And I oughta know. I'm the best of 'em."

On this point the Bakerman was not wrong. He could radically change and rearrange the chemistry of a party, a play, a crowd on the street, a relationship with another person, or a relationship between two people hosing on a couch in New York, which was the second occasion upon which I knew for sure someone was watching over me. Unfortunately, it had been the Bakerman both times, and unless the Bakerman was God, a possibility I was not quite ready to dismiss, I saw damn little evidence of a divine power monitoring our misbegotten moves along the sullen squares of the chessboard of life.

And so it was that soon after Abbie's appearance I left Ratso's apartment. Like a bird of the sixties, I flew that sordid cage. Like a dove or an eagle or a pigeon from Hawaii, I now found myself flying beneath the radar, riding the couch circuit, buying cigars from Village Cigars on Seventh Avenue, in ever larger quantities, snorting weasel-dust, in ever larger quantities, at the Monkey's Paw in Sheridan Square, hanging out with my old ramblin' boy the Bakerman on the streets and the sidewalks of New York, and sadly coming to the realization by the tawdry tail feathers of the seventies that the bird of the sixties had flown.

I took a place on Vandam Street. It was a sparsely furnished loft on the second floor of an old, decrepit warehouse recently converted to the Church of the Latter-Day Landlord, but it was home to me. It also soon became a sometime sanctuary for Abbie, a hotel and halfway house for the Bakerman, and a place where Judy would, on occasion, come spiritually slumming. My initial paranoia at having Abbie peripatetically crashing at the place soon insinuated itself into the raw, ubiquitous paranoia of the times. But Abbie was good company when he was around and Ratso was flipping over the heat, real or imagined, from the feds. Except for Baker's voyeuristic observation of Judy and myself on Ratso's couch, none of my three occasional housepests could be said to have known each other.

Basically, it was a lonely place. You could stand out on the rusty fire-escape landing and look at other rusty fire escapes, dirty brick walls, garbage trucks, two-legged rats, broken streetlights, and dark-colored pigeons. Lots and lots of nothing but nothing. You could sit on some kind of a crazy orange crate chair that was like falling off the end of the world and look at the little snapshot of Kacey as a child at the airport in Canada with the same eyes that Marilyn Monroe had looked at her little picture of Abraham Lincoln she always kept on her bedside table. But Kacey had kissed her last windshield and nobody was up in the balcony masturbating to Marilyn anymore and Lincoln must've been the first Jewish president because he'd gotten shot in the temple. That left only me and the cockroaches, but at least there would never be a problem getting up a *minion*.

One night I was standing by a broken floor lamp just smoking a cigar and listening to my hair grow when the shit really hit the radiator. The radiator, fortunately, had not been working at the time. Neither, of course, had I.

16

"Was that what I thought it was?" said Tom, stumbling blearily out of the bedroom.

"Had to be either a gunshot or Mama Cass farting," I said, moving quickly over to the window.

"Stay away from the windows."

"That's what Abbie told me when he thought somebody'd followed him to Ratso's place."

"Now *I'm* tellin' you. Whoever followed him to Ratso's by now could've followed him here. There's a lot of people, so I hear, who wouldn't mind blowing him away. So use your head for something besides a hat rack. When you hear a gunshot in the street, stay the hell away from the fucking windows."

"What if he's lying in the street bleeding to death?"

"Did he tell you he was coming by tonight?"

"He never tells me dick. He just materializes."

"Then it just could've been the usual cowboys and Indians," said Baker, as he crept up on the window. "I don't see anything out there. Anyway we can't call the cops with all this Irving Berlin's White Christmas lying around here."

"Not to mention weasel-dust."

"I doubt if there's enough cocaine in that weasel-dust to warrant an arrest."

"Tell that to my left nostril."

"What the hell was that?" said Tom as another shot echoed off the canyons of Vandam Street. This was followed moments later by a scream that seemed to emanate from directly below my second-floor window.

"Holy Moly!" said Baker. "There *is* a fucking cowboy down there! He's wearing a big black hat just like yours."

"One of us will have to leave the party," I said.

I moved closer to Baker's large form by the window and peered down into the darkness of Vandam Street. The vision that I saw was not calculated to spread joy to the souls of people who place a high priority on property values. Of course people who place a high priority on property values usually don't have a hell of a lot of soul to begin with. A soul is something you can't own; you can only rent it by fucking up your life enough to reach a state of what Nelson Algren called "achieved innocence," like a prostitute who gives her money to her boyfriend. Another way to get soul is to let a half-crazed Abbie Hoffman, dressed in high rodeo drag, come up to your loft.

"Who is that guy?" asked Baker. "What the hell does he want?"

"It's Abbie Hoffman," I said.

"He looks like a Jewish meatball in a cowboy hat," said the Bakerman, suddenly seeing great humor in the situation. "Better let him in before this turns into a *Gunsmoke* rerun."

One of the things I loved about the Bakerman was his total absence of fear. He did things with reckless abandon, thinking of only what was the right or the wrong thing to do and doing both in just about equal measure, never reflecting upon the consequences of his actions. It was an attractive trait if you could get away with it. And Baker had been smart, tough, talented, and lucky enough to do just that. So far.

Before I knew it the Bakerman was out the door and down the stairs. From the window I watched him corral Abbie and drag him through the front door of the building. Moments later they were both safely inside the loft, Abbie frisbeeing his cowboy hat against the far wall in anger and disgust.

"Fucking disguise didn't fool him," he said.

"Nice to meet you, Abbie," said Baker, watching the hat roll back across the floor.

"Barry Freed," said Abbie, extending his hand to Baker.

"Chuck Hitler," said the Bakerman winking broadly at me.

"Well," I said, "now that we all know each other, what do we do if the police arrive?"

"Offer 'em a line," said the Bakerman.

He followed this statement by snorting a large line himself off the kitchen table, then offering one to Abbie. Abbie declined, as I suspected he would. It was mildly ironic, because the trumped-up charges against him dealt with possession of cocaine, a drug I'd never known Abbie to use. He would smoke pot, however, and he would take a drink, which I now proceeded to offer him.

I'd kind of liked the Jameson Irish Whiskey Kurt had poured for Cleve and myself at the Lone Star, so I'd recently bought a bottle and I opened it and poured three long shots into three mismatched, chipped, and stained coffee cups that represented all the china I currently had in the loft. Baker and I toasted Abbie.

"To the sixties," I said.

"To the sixties," said Abbie. "When the drugs were cheap, the love was free, and the music was great!"

"Hear! Hear!" said the Bakerman, raising an eyebrow in Abbie's direction.

We killed the shots and I quickly poured each of us another drink. I raised my cup in a toast.

"To the seventies," I said.

"Fuck the seventies," said Abbie.

"I won't drink to that," said the Bakerman.

"Why not?" I asked.

"They ain't worth fucking."

Baker then launched into some kind of Irish drinking song that kept repeating the phrase "We'll get a bloody rope and we'll hang the fucking pope," possibly lifted from Patrick Sky's album *Songs That Made America Famous* or possibly quite a bit older. I didn't really know a lot about the Irish. I just knew the Bakerman, the song "Kevin Barry," and the recently formulated belief that Jameson's had probably kept the Irish from taking over the world. For a Texas Jewboy, it wasn't a bad start.

"It was the same guy," said Abbie, glancing toward the window. "The same guy who followed me to Ratso's place a few weeks ago. The bastard's persistent, I'll give him that. If it hadn't been for all the garbage trucks blocking his line of vision he probably would've drilled me. You can't call the law when you're running from the law. I need to find out who this guy is. I need your help, Kinkela."

"You mean," said the Bakerman, "it's all up to Finky, I mean Stinky, I mean Pinky, I mean Kinky?"

"I'm not a private dick," I said.

"You can say that again," said Baker.

"But you can help me, Kinkela," said Abbie. "You've got the mind of a modern-day Sherlock Holmes."

I looked at Tom Baker. He shrugged a friendly, somewhat theatrical shrug and laughed to himself.

"Who gave you *that* brilliant idea?" I asked.

"You're the modern-day Sherlock Holmes," said Abbie. "Figure it out."

"I think I have," I said.

17

The following afternoon I was killing time and pain at a nearby bar called The Ear, so named because the two ribs of the "B" in the neon sign that read "Bar" had burned out years ago. So had most of the patrons. I was waiting for Judy but thinking about Abbie. For a guy with the "mind of a modern-day Sherlock Holmes" I was having a hell of a time figuring out how I could possibly help my fugitive friend. Ratso, of course, had put the idea in his head, but he seemed to believe it, and that had me mildly worried. At least two Americans, obviously, had more faith in me than I had in myself.

Not that I didn't want to help Abbie. Indeed, Baker and I had ventured out later that night on a reconnaissance tour of Vandam Street and found no gunman, no shell casings, no stranger lurking in the shadows except an old bum asking for a handout. I gave him a sawbuck and he said, "God bless the both of youse." I don't know whether God blessed me and the Bakerman or not. We didn't see Him on Vandam Street either.

For his part, Abbie slept it off and rode out early in the morning, leaving his cowboy hat behind in the dust. I wondered again if anybody had really been following Abbie. Or could it be that he was so paranoid and self-absorbed by this time that he'd merely heard gunshots in the New York night and misinterpreted them as intended for him? Anything was possible in this best of all possible worlds. What was impossible was for me to locate and identify his pursuer if said pursuer didn't exist. Even Sherlock would've required more than three pipefuls to solve that one.

The other annoying question was how could I help Abbie when I was barely able to help myself? Marching powder prices were going up all the time and the cheaper—and gnarlier—weasel-dust was not always available. Jameson Irish Whiskey, cigars, and occasional food also created financial, not to mention emotional, problems, especially since Bill Dick was not providing me with a king's ransom to play the Lone Star once a week.

As far as human relationships went, and that's rarely very far, the friends I currently had were not the kind you could really lean on very hard. Ratso was busy reading his ten thousand books on Hitler, Bob Dylan, and Jesus; Abbie was busy running from his own shadow; the Bakerman was busy fighting demons the nature of which I could only guess in a nightmare; and Judy was busy being late to meet me here at The Ear. So I ordered another shot of Jameson's and watched Martin the bartender languidly wash the glasses as he languidly watched a rerun of *Ironside* on TV. Where the hell were the Watergate hearings when you needed them? I wondered.

Where the hell was Judy? Where was Kacey?

I wandered into the men's room of The Ear, a facility which made its counterpart at the Monkey's Paw seem and smell positively upscale by comparison, and retrieved a small tin foil packet from the pocket of my old blue winter coat, which looked like a hand-me-down from Oliver Twist. In the time it took to open the packet, double-check the security of the rather flimsy door, place a large gob of weasel-dust on the end of a house key, and lever the whole operation to the vicinity of my left nostril, many questions raced through my frazzled mind. Why was a bright, talented, young man like myself snorting weasel-dust in the middle of the afternoon in the men's room of The Ear when I was just attaining what should have been the Prime of Miss Kinky Friedman? Why wasn't I leaving a suburban home in a shiny new four-wheeled penis with two kids, Winston and Kool, whining about McDonald's and the weather-beaten wife whining about Neiman-Mucous? Just lucky, I guess.

Then I took a huge snort of the weasel-dust and the naked tip of the house key glinted like a Pakistani moon and I saw the green flash that you sometimes see when the sun sets in Hawaii and suddenly there were no thoughts or questions in my head at all. Instead, there was within the inner ear of The Ear a certain edgy, endless, earthbound hum like the sound you hear when you first come to New York and you're trying to sleep and you haven't learned how to ignore it yet like you've learned to ignore almost everything else you learned as a child. Then the hum itself was interrupted by a sudden staccato hammering sound. I quickly refolded the tinfoil and thrust it back in my pocket.

“Open up that door, buddy!” a voice shouted. “I gotta whiz like a racehorse!”

“Give me another twenty-five minutes,” I said. “I’m squirtin’ out of both ends.”

“That’s all right, buddy,” said the stranger. “I’ll take a leak in the alley.”

“You’re a fine American,” I said.

As I heard his footsteps rapidly shuffling away I took the tinfoil packet out again and this time used the corner of a matchbook to fork a double blast into my heretofore neglected right nostril. Nothing happened. No hum of brain cells frying or green flashes or projectile diarrhea. Nothing. It was the rain-barrel effect in which, after so much has happened to you, nothing makes any difference any more, which of course leads to the Swiss-cheese effect, in which you can’t remember why you were in the dumper in the first place. None of this was very healthy, nor did it make me proud to be an American to think that, because of my depravity, some guy was, at this very moment, freezing his dick off in the alley.

By the time I got back to the bar, Martin was still washing glasses, *Ironside* was over, and Judy was standing there looking highly agitato with her mascara running like dirty New York raindrops.

“What’s the matter?” I said. “Your guppies die?”

“Where the hell have you been?” she said.

“Had a little projectile diarrhea,” I said. “What’s it to you?”

“I just saw a face,” she said. Her own face was whiter than Klansmen’s sheets.

“That’s a good lyric for a song,” I said. “Was the face attached to a guy with his pecker out who was taking a whiz like a racehorse?"

"No. The face was attached to a body with two legs and when he saw me he ran away."

"The guy with the pecker. Did he try to run away, too?"

"No," she said, starting up the waterworks again.

"That's a blessing," I said. "Pecker tracks on your trousers can be quite a social embarrassment."

"I'm serious, Kinky. I think I'm going crazy."

"See a shrink," I said, striving for a light tone.

"I *am* seeing a shrink," said Judy quietly. "His name is Dr. Bock. I've been seeing him for four months."

"Tell him you want your money back."

Indeed, Judy's eyes did look like those of the Mad Lady of Chaillot. This might be more serious than I'd thought. I turned to Martin and ordered us both a round of drinks to settle her down.

"No," she said emphatically. "You come out to the alley with me now to see if he's still lurking about."

"I thought the guy spooked you and you wanted to get away from him."

"He *did* spook me. But I think I know who he is."

Before I could inquire further, Judy had pivoted on her shapely wheels and headed for the door with me right behind her. Whoever was out there, I didn't want her going into the alley by herself. I didn't even want to go into the alley by *myself.* But, being one of the very few southern gentlemen in New York, I had no choice.

The only sign of recent human habitation in the alley was a large fresh urine stain on a nearby brick wall. Obviously, the guy with the pecker. Judy looked around and I looked around and we wandered together to where the alley met the little street behind The Ear, but we didn't see anything that could be termed suspish. I was frankly wondering if Judy had been taking Abbie Hoffman lessons. I was also considering recommending Dr. Bock to Abbie. He'd done such a good job with Judy that her brain seemed to be going into automatic transmission.

"I don't understand it," she said. "It can't be."

"What can't be?"

"He was standing here a few minutes ago."

"So he ran away."

"But you're missing the point. Ratso said you had the mind—"

"Of a modern-day Sherlock Holmes?"

"That's right. He said you could solve any mystery if you put your mind to it."

"The only mystery is why anybody listens to Ratso."

"Don't you understand why I'm shaking, why I'm crying, why I'm so upset?"

"Look," I said, "why don't you come on over to my place and we'll make love on my karate mat."

"But he was standing right *here.*"

"*Who* was standing right here?"

"Tim," she said. "I saw *Tim.*"

18

Of course I didn't have a karate mat. What I had, apparently, was a moderately psycho girlfriend, so I brought her over for a little counseling session on the mattress on the floor of the bedroom. The mattress had been there when I subtlet the loft and God knows how long before that, and, no doubt, it had some rather wiggy stories to tell. So did Judy.

To put it on a bumper sticker for you, she claimed to have seen her former flyboy lover Tim in the alley, a man whose remains she'd personally witnessed being buried a little over seven months before. Now she'd seen Tim, he'd seen her, then he'd run away and disappeared down the alley. Judy was sure she was crazy. I didn't argue with her. I just gave her a checkup from the neck up and then a thorough and fastidious checkup just about everywhere else. Needless to say, I wasn't a shrink. I wasn't even a detective. All I can tell you is she was easy on the lips.

The same Lord who'd delivered white pigeons to Hawaii

and dark pigeons to New York also had provided for Tom Baker and Abbie Hoffman to be out of the loft that evening. The divine plan for once meshed pretty well with my own plans, and when Judy left the loft sometime early the next morning both of us were in a little better frame of mind. Judy was convinced she'd seen a vision that had an important message to impart to her. I was convinced that I had an important message to impart to Ratso.

As the dawn's surly light drifted into the loft, I put on my old purple Robert Louis Stevenson house robe and wandered into my ill-equipped kitchen. The only cooking implement in the place was an old-fashioned coffee percolator that Tom Baker had brought over in the misguided notion that that would be his contribution to the rent situation. It looked like the kind of ancient device the Lone Ranger might've placed on the campfire after he'd stirred the coals with Tonto's penis.

Baker had also brought with him to the loft a small bag of French roast coffee and a similar-looking small bag of Peruvian marching powder. The difference was that one was black and one was white. I put a small portion of the black one into the percolator and I put a small portion of the white one into my left nostril. Soon the percolator was humming along almost as well as I was.

I had one cigar left from the handful I'd bought at Village Cigars recently and I lit that booger up and paced back and forth across the empty living room of the loft as I waited for the percolator to catch up with me. The first thing I had to do, I figured, was to buy Ratso a muzzle for Christmas. Christmas, of course, had come and gone some time ago without a whimper. The only thing I liked about Christmas was that it raised the possibility of hearing Willie Nelson sing "Pretty Papers" or Jimmy Durante sing "Frostie the Snowman." Everything else about the whole cloying, tedious season you could roll in suppository form, as far as I was concerned, and you could fly. The only holiday I cared for very much was Shevuoth. I didn't know why it was celebrated but I liked the way it sounded. Also, very few people chose Shevuoth-time in which to take a Brodie.

I had another hit of the marching powder for the right nostril and found that it almost blew the back of my head off. It was far superior to the weasel-dust of the night before. What did the Weasel put in that crap anyway? Could be almost anything. The blood of little Christian children? The blood of little Jewish children? How would you ever know the difference?

When the coffee was ready, I poured myself a cup and took it and the cigar over to a yellow, battle-scarred hassock that looked like it'd been left over from the set of *The Adventures of Ozzie and Harriet.* I sat down, balanced the coffee on my knee, and brooded about the way Ratso's proselytizing on my behalf had screwed up and complicated my otherwise totally meaningless existence. Something had to be done about it, and soon, before every neurotic nerd in New York was coming to me with his troubles.

I was sipping the coffee, puffing on the cigar, and steeling my last nerve to call Ratso, when the phone rang. I walked over to the rickety end table where the telephone resided and picked up the blower.

"Start talkin'," I said.

"Kinkstah!" shouted the loud, familiar-sounding, rodent-like voice. "Kinkstah!"

"Up jumped the devil," I said.

"Better the devil you know."

I put the cigar down in a nearby Cadillac hubcap the Bakerman had found in his recent travels and took a little time to choose my words carefully.

"Fuckhead," I said. "I think the two of us should get together to discuss my brilliant career as a detective."

"Great, Sherlock! I knew you'd come around. You've been too modest about your prowess. When do you want to meet?"

"Now."

"Okay, Sherlock! Come on over," said Ratso, cheerfully oblivious to the undercurrent of anger in my voice.

"Why don't you come over here? After all, Mrs. Hudson was Holmes's housekeeper and Hudson Street is much closer to Vandam than it is to your place."

"Makes sense to me, Sherlock."

"I was afraid you'd think so."

"Is this about Barry Freed?"

"Could be. Just get your buttocks over here will you?"

"Sure thing, Sherlock! Can't wait to see how you've fixed up your new place."

I looked around me at the Bakerman's castle of empty beer cans, the dust, the dirt, the heartbreaking emptiness of this station-on-the-way to Desolation Row.

"Well," I said, "it's not yet ready for *Architectural Digest.*"

"From what I hear," said Ratso, with a gleeful, squirrel-like chuckle, "it's not yet ready for *Reader's Digest.*"

I hung up the blower and walked over to a window and watched garbage trucks for a while. Ratso had a good heart, I thought, and he did possess some sense of responsibility. After all, he'd recently been appointed editor of *High Times* magazine, a publication that was currently in the toilet in terms of readership and circulation, not to mention content. Ratso's job was to keep the magazine in the toilet until management could decide what to do with it. He took his job very seriously.

To Ratso's credit as an editor, however, was the fact that at his behest I'd written my first prose piece for the magazine. The article, based loosely upon my Peace Corps experiences, had been entitled "My Scrotum Flew Tourist: A Personal Odyssey."

But being a detective of any sort, I reflected, was a wholly different matter bearing a different level of responsibility. To be a detective is to be a mender of destinies. To be a detective is to look inside other people's fears and secrets and hopes and dreams. Dreams can never hurt you, I thought, as I walked back toward the percolator and the cocaine.

Only the dreamers can.

19

After several hours of waiting for Ratso in an empty, ennui-laden loft, I was about ready to hang myself from the shower rod. It was at about that time that I discovered that there wasn't any shower rod. Walking back into the living room in near despair, I had another realization. Jumping out of a second-floor window and almost certainly landing on top of a garbage truck, while making for a rather humorous, ignominious obit, was hardly a precise method of topping yourself. Very likely you'd only paralyze yourself and then you'd have to watch every sanctimonious, guilt-ridden asshole you've ever known in your life, each one in a spirit of secret glee, drop by with a fruit basket.

I was roused from these somewhat morbid reflections by what sounded like the shriek of a wounded faggot. I walked over to the window and observed Ratso dressed in a silver lamé outfit that looked like a cross between Liberace and the first Jewish astronaut, Nose Cone. It was a strange but not entirely unwelcome sight. Indeed I was almost mildly wavering about the notion of becoming a detective when I grew up. But to be a detective, first you've got to have something to detect. The only thing I was detecting now was that Ratso was becoming increasingly cold and highly agitato standing there on the sidewalk.

I opened the window and shouted to him that I'd be right down.

"Why don't you just jump?" he shouted back, not realizing how close he'd come to my true thoughts moments earlier. Most people don't realize it when they come close to the truth. That's why most people keep going.

I kept going myself, out the door of the loft, down one flight of stairs, down another, through the shabby little lobby where a bum who could've been me ten years from now was huddled in a corner dreaming of the Big Rock Candy Mountain, and on out to Vandam Street. Ratso, I noticed upon closer inspection, was wearing his coonskin cap with the little creature's head sewn on the front, eyes sewn shut.

"You look like Davy Crockett drowning in bull semen," I said, holding the front door open for Ratso.

"I *feel* like Davy Crockett drowning in bull semen after standing on the sidewalk shouting for twenty minutes. How'd this guy get in so easily?" said Ratso, motioning toward the sleeping bum.

"He's the doorman," I said.

We climbed the stairs together and had hardly gotten in the door before Ratso began feigning an interior decorator's excitement upon seeing the hideously depressing, stark, dirty, unfurnished loft.

"*Love* it!" he ejaculated. "It's so *you*!"

"Ratso," I said, "I'd just like to—"

"That frog umbrella stand makes my *eyes* burn!"

"Baker lifted that from someplace. It's about the last possession I need on this planet. What I'd really like to talk about—"

"And all this lovely exposed brick and dark, cool Egyptian-tomb ambience," said Ratso, twirling around now like the woman in *The Sound of Music.*

"Goddammit, Ratso—"

"And what have we *here*?" he cooed, gazing questioningly into the bedroom, which had nothing going for it but a mattress on the floor and an exposed lightbulb and resembled more than anything a jail cell in Turkey.

"Early crash-pad decor," he continued. "Charmingly understated. Maybe over there in the corner a lava lamp might be nice—"

"I'm not Sherlock Holmes!" I shouted. *"You're not Dr. Watson!"*

Ratso turned and looked at me with the sudden, disarming eyes of a child who's just been informed there is no Santa Claus. Ignoring his gaze, I plodded on.

"This was just a little game we played, but don't you see, Ratso, now we're playing with *real lives.*"

"I know," said Ratso. "It's more fun this way."

"Look, Rats, it's bad enough you've got Abbie thinking—"

"Barry Freed."

"Okay. The legendary what's-his-name. It's bad enough you've got him thinking I'm his personal savior in this matter. The guy's totally frazzled from years as a fugitive and hopelessly paranoid and there's probably nobody following him anyway. That would be bad enough, but you weren't satisfied. Now you've got Judy convinced that I've got 'the mind of a modern-day Sherlock Holmes' and you didn't realize that she's been going to a shrink. Now she thinks she's seeing her dead boyfriend—"

"The one from the Jefferson Airplane?"

"—and she thinks I'm the only one who can help her."

"Maybe she's right. Look, Sherlock—"

"Stop saying that."

"Okay. Look, Kinkstah—"

"Stop saying that, too."

"Okay. Look, asshole. You've got two of your friends who think they're in trouble. They may be crazy. They may *not* be crazy. There may be one case here. There may be two cases. There may be nothing. The very least you can do is keep a watchful eye on them and see what happens."

"The very least you can do is pull your lips together."

"Let me just finish and then I'll be out of here."

"Good."

"You're a lot more like Sherlock than you think and I don't just mean the way your mind works. I mean the kind of person you are. You're an outwardly cold person with a heart of gold, just like Sherlock."

"Give it a rest, Ratso."

"You're lonely and you live in a lonely place. This loft gives me the creeps. You ought to at least get a pet or something. Maybe a dog or a bird. Or how about an iguana, like the one they just put up on top of the Lone Star? Iguanas are very trendy right now."

"Ratso, I'm beggin' you to stop."

"I'm almost through. You and Sherlock both were cocaine addicts when you weren't working. You both were your own severest critics. You both often doubted your own abilities. You both constantly felt sorry for yourselves. You both were subject to serious bouts of depression. And you both, very likely, were latent homosexuals."

"And you, very likely, are a latent schmuck. There's a couple things you and Dr. Watson have in common now that I think about it. You were both nerds and neither of you ever understood a fucking thing."

"Just promise me you'll keep a close eye on Judy and Abbie."

"You mean Barry Freed."

"Promise you'll keep an eye on them and then we'll see if anything develops."

"And if something does?"

"Then, Sherlock," said Ratso, dancing triumphantly around the loft again, "the game is afoot!"

Ratso left the loft moments later in what was as close to a huff as someone dressed like him could possibly engender. I watched from the window as he walked away down Vandam Street.

20

That Sunday night, in a freezing drizzle with guitar in hand, I hailed a hack at the corner of Vandam and Hudson. I had a gig to do and I figured Bill Dick would like it if I got there on time for once. I'd recently changed the name of the band from the Shalom Retirement Village People to something a bit more sexy—the Exxon Brothers—but I knew the weekly gig at the Lone Star coupled with the occasional New Jersey bar-mitzvah party was not a career. Hell, it wasn't even what you'd call a living. All it was was another show in my hip pocket.

"Lone Star Cafe," I said to the cabbie, as I shlepped the guitar into the back seat with me.

"Okay, buddy," said the driver. "You're sure it ain't the Russian Tea Room?"

"Do I look like a Russian?"

"In this town, who can tell? Where's your horse?"

"It passed away."

The cabbie was a real New Yorker. We'd gone one block and he knew my life story. New Yorkers, of course, have always liked to poke fun at cowboys and cowboys have always liked to poke fun at New Yorkers and it's just a wonder no one ever gets pissed off. If they did, you wouldn't know it. In this town, who could tell?

"With all this rain," he said, as we waited interminably at a red light, "it's a good thing you brought your ten-gallon hat."

"Yeah," I said. "Now if I could just get a little cocktail umbrella for my cigar."

"You know J.R. on *Dallas?*"

"Not personally."

"Somebody oughta shoot that guy."

"We could dig up Lee Harvey Oswald and use him as a hand puppet."

"Now you're talkin', pal."

What happened next is kind of hard to describe. I saw a hand reach out for the handle of the right-side passenger door of the hack. The hand was attached to an army jacket above which a black ski mask completely covered the head and face. Before I knew what was happening, the driver took off like a rocket ship through the red light. A crosstown bus came barreling toward us in oncoming traffic. Seconds before it would've T-boned the taxi, the cabbie scooted across the street.

"Jay-zuz Christ!" shouted the cabbie.

"What the hell're you doing?" I said.

"Guy had a gun."

"I didn't see any gun."

"Guy had a gun. Maybe he took one look at you and thought we were a stagecoach."

"I didn't see any—"

This thought was interrupted by a slightly muffled but very close-to-home noise that sounded like a kid was shooting off a popgun inside my head. Almost at the same time the back window of the cab blew out, showering both of us with glass and rain and a little bit of red stuff that seemed to be emanating from the back of my neck.

I took off my hat, crouched low in the seat, and peered carefully out what was left of the back window. I thought I saw a guy running away with a large black gun in his hand but with the rain and the traffic and the darkness it was hard to tell.

"You okay, buddy?" asked the cabbie.

"May the heavens kiss my balls," I said. "It's just a scratch."

"Fortunately, I rent the cab, but nobody rents their head, pal. I don't know what this town is coming to! It's like the goddamn ol' West! Terrorism everywhere! You want I should take you to St. Vincent's?"

"No, just take me to the mental hospital," I said. "Lone Star Cafe."

I did the show on automatic pilot that night. I hardly remember being on stage, though Baker told me later it was one of my better performances. Whether he was serious or not I'll probably never know. No one ever knows whether the Bakerman is serious. That's part of his charm.

I was having a beer with him after the second show, up in the dressing room, and he suggested we go out on the roof and see the iguana. I'd been so stunned by the hack attack that I hadn't even noticed the huge monster lurching out over Fifth Avenue when I'd come in the place. Now, with spotlights shining all over its green scales, it looked positively otherworldly.

"Bill Dick must've changed his mind or killed himself," I said. "He claimed this iguana would go up here over his dead body."

"He's not exactly Mr. Charismo," said Baker. "How would we know?"

"Somebody's signing my checks."

"Somebody's taking potshots at you, too. I almost lost my meal ticket and my best friend at the same time tonight. I'm not exactly fartin' through silk these days. You may have noticed. Times are getting tough, Kinky, and I'm getting tired of this wicked world. I ran into a bartender down the street tonight who was the very first friend I had when I came to New York years ago. You may be my last."

Tom Baker's Irish eyes, which had so often smiled with a world-beating lust for life, now seemed to shine with a righteous sadness. I could see broken American dreams, ruins of an older, more graceful civilization. How much can you read into a dear friend's eyes? How much is merely a reflection of yourself? You never find the answers to those questions before the final exam. Maybe next time, I thought.

"This obviously isn't the way to the men's dumper," said a voice in the darkness.

I looked up and saw Steve Rambam, the rabbinical student who'd given the cop so much hell over the parking ticket. Dressed in a suit and tie and balancing a beer on one of the iguana's left hind toenails, he looked for all the world like a successful stockbroker.

"You said to drop by some time," said Rambam. "Here I am."

I introduced Tom and Steve and then Tom wandered back into the club, offering the two of us the following little farewell speech before he left.

"Well, I'll leave you girls out here to get acquainted. By the way, Steve, if Kinky looks like he's cookin' on another planet it's just because somebody tried to kill him tonight. And now, as Sam Cooke said at the Copacabana: 'I don't wanta go, but I gotta go.'"

"Nice exit," said Rambam.

"Baker's a very colorful American."

"I'm talking about the one you almost made. You know I've enrolled in the police academy as well as the yeshiva. Tell me what happened."

Rambam looked trustworthy, cocky, and confident, and besides, I needed someone to talk to, so I told him about the incident with the taxicab. That led naturally to Abbie and the guy he thought was following him and the gunshots several nights back. I used the name "Barry Freed" and described him merely as "an old friend with a somewhat checkered past." This description, of course, could've applied to almost anyone I knew. For good measure I threw in Ratso's indefatigable campaign to bring our little Holmes-Watson game kicking and screaming into the stark, cold casino of reality. As icing on the cake that someone left out in the rain, I mentioned Judy's recent sighting of her dead boyfriend and her subsequent appeal to the court of last resort, Sherlock Holmes aka the Kinkster. Rambam sipped his beer and thought it over for a while. He shook his head several times almost to himself and then he spoke.

"Being Sherlock Holmes can be dangerous," he said, "even if you don't wear a deerstalker or play the violin."

"I'm not Sherlock Holmes, for Christ's sake."

"Tell that to Ratso and Barry Freed and Judy," he said. "And maybe somebody else."

"It's the somebody else I'm worried about."

"Here's what I can do," said Rambam, standing up abruptly. "I've got a little time off now and I can stake out your place and watch the comings and goings of your friend Barry Freed and maybe follow whoever's following him. As far as your friend Judy is concerned, I've also applied for medical school and I can tell you she sounds quite delusional, though, of course, I haven't met her. I can dig around a bit with the Graves Registration Unit of the Navy and maybe we can put her flyboy to rest once and for all. As far as your friend Ratso's concerned, he may have unintentionally put you in the line of fire earlier tonight. He seems quite persistent and, no doubt, well-intentioned, and that combination is nearly always poison. I'll get in touch with you because we may need to work together on some of this. It'll probably all turn out to be nothing. Mistaken identity or something like that."

"Thanks for your help, Steve," I said. "It was good to have someone to talk to."

"Don't mention it," he said. "We'll get to the bottom of this. In the meantime, there's only one thing you need to do."

"What's that?"

"Watch out for Reichenbach Falls," he said.

21

Whether I liked it or not, the previous night's unpleasant incident in the taxicab had suddenly made the game very real. I was now a player and there was no time to renegotiate my contract or ask to be traded. With Abbie snoring away like a band saw in the bedroom and Baker somewhere out on a bender, I made myself some coffee, sat down on the orange crate, and tried to face the cloud-shrouded New York morning with a cold, rational mind.

If I'd had a desk in the loft there certainly was an idea in my head that would've crossed it by this time. It was an old Indian trick actually. You spot a cowboy one night and he's wearing a black hat. You shoot and miss. Several moons later you see a cowboy in a black hat go by in a stagecoach and you shoot again. You figure this time you'll get him. Fortunately you miss again. Maybe you're a nearsighted Indian.

Obviously whoever had tried to croak Abbie the other night had mistaken me for him. There aren't very many cowboy hats in New York these days and when you spot one it will tend to make your trigger finger itch. Of course, Abbie might never wear a cowboy hat again in his life. For me, however, that was not the situation. The cowboy hat was an integral part of my high rodeo drag. Nor was it merely a sartorial matter. The cowboy hat was an essential component of my cultural heritage and my spiritual existence. All this notwithstanding, the time had very possibly come for me to heed Tom Baker's advice: use my head for something other than a hat rack.

Eighty-sixing the cowboy hat did not necessarily mean that I couldn't substitute a sky piece of another genre, of course. I could actually wear a deerstalker cap like Sherlock himself except that I'd look like an outpatient from Bellevue. Possibly wearing a yamaha on my head with a chin strap might be nice. Or I could check with Ratso about the feasibility of signing a long-term lease for his coonskin cap. Life was full of possibilities, I thought. Unfortunately, so was death.

In the bedroom behind me, Abbie was still snoring away. On the street just below, the garbage trucks were growling at each other in what sounded like a territorial battle royal. Vandam Street, apparently, was the territory they all desired. I walked over to the window in the little kitchen area and scanned the street for any sign of Rambam. There was nothing. I supposed, of course, if a stakeout was any good at all, it wouldn't be something you'd notice easily. Now that I was a detective of sorts I'd have to sharpen my powers of observation somewhat. What you see in this world is not always what you get.

The fact that somebody might mistake one Hebe in a cowboy hat, namely me, for another Hebe in a cowboy hat, namely Abbie, did not particularly fall into the brilliant deduction department. On the face of it, however, that was the way things stood at the moment. The other little thing that was bothering me was the aggressive nature of Abbie's pursuer. I now had to assume that the guy had been trying to croak Abbie when he'd shot at him on Vandam Street several nights ago. The guy had certainly been trying to croak me. Unless you consider somebody blowing the back window out of the taxicab you're riding in to be a warning shot. Regardless of Abbie's insistence that the feds were after him, I had to wonder about the nature of the nemesis. Would a federal agent behave in such a reckless, lethal fashion?

After pondering matters for a while longer, I found that I was developing a natural craving for a cigar, which I didn't have, and for a solution, which I didn't have either. The stress of all this deductive reasoning appeared to be taking its toll upon my gray-matter department, not to mention that it seemed to be exacerbating my propensity toward projectile diarrhea. So I took a little break and turned on the Bakerman's old beat-up radio and that was how I learned that Imus was no longer in the morning.

"What the hell do you mean he's not there?" I shouted at the woman who answered the phone at the radio station.

"Just what I said, sir. He's no longer with the station."

"That's impossible," I said. "He's been there forever."

"Not anymore, sir," she said rather curtly.

"Well, if he's not there," I said, "then where the hell is he?"

"Try Cleveland," said the woman.

"You try Cleveland," I said, but the woman, apparently, had already cradled the blower.

It was beyond my imagination. Imus had been a spiritual and sometimes financial linchpin of my life in New York. His morning radio show had both made him a cultural institution as well as leaving him virtually at the gates of a mental institution. His success was such that he could at any given moment send his limo out for cocaine. This trait made him even more attractive to the Kinkster, not to mention his abiding friendship and his terminally ill sense of humor.

But Imus did have one little problem. I don't know if you consider a man who drinks a large tropical fish aquarium full of vodka a day an alcoholic or not. Certainly it's not morally wrong. If you have an outrageous reputation as a truth-teller, a lot of talent, a limo, and a top-rated radio show, you might get away with it forever. It's just that sooner or later everyone and everything in your life appears to be moving by on a motorized tie rack with the express purpose of cutting into your cocktail hour.

This apparently is what had happened to Imus. Of course I wasn't Imus and alcohol wasn't cocaine, but I could see the writing on the men's-room wall as well as I could still see Imus in my mind, passed out on the floor of the men's room, wearing Eric Clapton's famous jacket, which I myself had given him. Eric no doubt wouldn't have minded. He'd been there before. As I recall Imus himself hadn't minded. He'd been there before, too. So that night I watched them pour him into the limo and send him home to his penthouse, and he was on the air the next morning, and people started to think he was funny when he was serious and serious when he was funny, and that's usually the beginning of the end. Then management became concerned. Then the people who bought his old house in Greenwich, Connecticut, reported that a boxcar full of empty vodka bottles had apparently derailed in their backyard. And now Imus had gone to Cleveland.

I turned off the radio.

With half-damp eyes I took my little Imus in the Morning coffee cup out of my busted valise. The cup had a little chip on its shoulder. So did Imus, of course. I was placing it on the windowsill, where it might get some sun, I suppose, when somebody tapped me on the shoulder and I damn near jumped through my asshole for America. I turned to see the dark, tortured eyes of Abbie Hoffman corkscrewing into my own.

"When you guys were gone last night," he said grimly, "somebody called me here."

"Sounds like your social life is picking up," I said. "How'd they get the number? I've only had the phone about a week."

"They have their ways. It was a guy calling in a death threat."

"Cast your mind back to last night. Exactly what were the caller's words?"

"'You Jew bastard. I'll kill you.'"

"Any idea who the caller was?"

"Not a clue," said Abbie. "But I'm not the detective. Who do *you* think it could be?"

"Well, given this kind of evidence," I said, "I always like to start by ruling out Sandy Koufax."

22

"So who is this Rambam character?" asked Ratso later that afternoon as the two of us sat at the Carnegie Deli eating pickles, drinking Dr. Brown's Black Cherry Soda, and waiting for two sandwiches that we fully anticipated would be bigger than our heads.

"He's just a young guy I met on the street the other night. But I like his style. He was involved in a little tension convention with a beat cop named Cooperman, I think, who gave him a parking ticket, but before that happened Rambam did manage to push him around like a little red apple. He's in rabbinical school, he's enrolled in the police academy, and he's currently applying to medical school."

"Sounds like the Jewish version of a butcher, a baker, and an Indian chief."

"Candlestick-maker," I said. "That's a butcher, a baker, and a candlestick-maker. And we may need a candlestick-maker if Rambam doesn't catch this guy in this stakeout. We'll have to pray this crazy bastard doesn't try to croak me again thinking I'm Abbie."

"Barry Freed," said Ratso.

"Anyway, I invited Rambam to join us here, so he should be showing up in a while. He said he'd be staking out the place, but I've been looking for him all morning and haven't seen hide nor hair of the boy."

"What do you think a stakeout looks like?" said Ratso, working away diligently on pickle number seven.

"Oh, you know, a guy slouched down with a fedora drinking coffee in a car. Eats a donut about every twenty minutes. Smokes a cigarette now and then."

"No," said Ratso. "That's bullshit. That's Hollywood brainwashing us all to believe that Rock Hudson and Doris Day are the perfect couple and everything ends happily ever after and all you have to do to see a stakeout is look out the window. You can only see a bad, uncreative stakeout. If your friend Rambam's any good he could've been staking out the place all morning. You'd never see him. A good stakeout's like God."

"Then let's put it this way," I said, looking around in vain for our waiter, "I don't believe there's a Rambam."

At this critical juncture my friend Leo Steiner, the engagingly brilliant pastrami purveyor and owner of the Carnegie, stopped by our table. Leo was always busy but he always had time for a friend.

"Kinky! Ratso! How you guys doin'? What? They didn't give you linen?"

"Well," I said, "it's really no prob—"

"What the hell's goin' on here?" shouted Leo across the heads of the multitudes of Hebrews eating everything from bagels to borscht. "Give 'em linen!"

It should be noted that the average Carnegie Deli customer wipes cream cheese off his nose with paper napkins that bear the logo of Leo holding a huge plate of food and proclaiming: "I make a goooood sandwich." Only very special customers and friends of Leo Steiner ever receive the coveted linen napkins. The linen itself is merely sort of a spiritual status symbol. What's really valuable is the way the other customers look up at you momentarily from their matzoh-ball soup with expressions varying from mild puzzlement to grudging admiration to downright envy.

Several waiters, of course, rapidly materialized, one providing the linen with grave dignity, and the other shlepping along two sandwiches that were indeed larger than the heads of any customer in the place. The only head I'd ever seen bigger than a Carnegie Deli sandwich, I reflected very briefly, was the head of that Irish reporter I'd met at the Monkey's Paw. McGovern, I think the bartender had said.

"I'm very interested, Sherlock," said Ratso, in a voice loud enough to make sure he could be heard while he was eating, "in this threatening phone call. This 'Jew bastard' shit."

A lady seated nearby looked over at Ratso as if he were a cockroach. As if he were a cockroach, Ratso continued happily and quite obliviously eating away at his sandwich.

"Anti-Semitism everywhere you look, Kinkstah," said Ratso, finally acknowledging the lady who was still staring at him in disgust.

"Don't mind her," I said. "She's probably just jealous because we got linen."

"Seriously though," Ratso continued, "that kind of invective coupled with a lone gunman mistakenly shooting at you in a taxicab sure doesn't sound like a government operation."

"Ah, my dear Watson, there's no holding you back, is there? That's precisely the same thought that crossed my mind when these two dastardly deeds occurred. I asked our friend who he thought might be behind all this and he became strangely silent. I must speak to him again on this matter. Quite possibly there's something he's not telling us. These may well be deep waters, Watson."

"Speaking of which," said Ratso, "I could use some more seltzer water."

We continued to eat our sandwiches. We continued to wait for Rambam. The waiter continued to avoid our table.

"What about some virulently right-wing group," said Ratso, "that he might've offended back in the sixties?"

"That dog won't hunt, Watson. Whoever's after him now may well be unaware of his provocative past. Quite possibly he knows his victim only as Barry Freed. Otherwise, why resort to such risky and dangerous tactics? Why not simply blow his cover with the feds?"

"Brilliant, Sherlock! So really all we're dealing with is the last four or five years."

"Which is about as long as it's probably going to take you to get your seltzer water. By the way, do not reveal to Rambam, if he ever gets here, the true identity of Barry Freed. I don't really know him that well yet."

"But you do trust him?"

"Ah, Watson, the only people I truly trust are thee and me, and sometimes I'm not so sure about thee."

"One more question, Sherlock. Considering the recent case of mistaken identity, why are you wearing your hat?"

"Because, my dear Watson, like all the rest of us, I'm a creature of narrow habit."

"You certainly are," said Ratso. "Especially when it comes to belching and farting."

I let his remark slide and eventually our waiter came by, the seltzer water appeared, and not long after that, the check arrived. Ratso immediately launched into a rather extensive, meticulous charade concerning the packaging and preparation of the remainder of his sandwich to be taken out of the restaurant. Ratso feinted several times toward his pocket but I could tell he never seriously considered helping out with the check.

"What's the matter, Ratso?" I said, quoting Tom Baker. "You got fishhooks in your pockets?"

"No," said Ratso, smiling blamelessly. "I'm a creature of narrow habit."

Just as I was preparing to pony up the bucks for the check, two things occurred at once. Ratso decided he wanted cheesecake for dessert and Rambam entered the restaurant. I introduced Rambam to Ratso. The waiter brought the cheesecake and dutifully noted its addition to the bill.

"What'd you find out?" Ratso asked Rambam as he forked a dump-truck-load of the dessert into his mouth.

"Hey, pal," said Rambam, "I just started this morning. This could take days. I did see Kinky here come to his window about twenty-five times."

"That's funny," I said. "I never saw you."

"Sure you did," said Rambam. "I was the garbageman standing by the Dumpster."

"Jesus," I said. "Of course I saw you. Did you see anyone matching the descriptions of Barry Freed or the guy who's stalking him?"

"Your friend may, quite understandably, be spooked a bit. I saw him at the window once, but when I left to come here he still hadn't come out of the building. And there was no sign whatsoever of any guy with long blond hair or an army jacket lurking around. I did see that friend of yours I met at the Lone Star, Tom Baker, come in and out of the place a few times, and I did see a woman who matches the description of your girlfriend Judy enter the building and leave some time later. I also observed a nun, some kids playing hooky, two winos, a guy in a wheelchair, a few other garbagemen, a cop, and Tom and Judy walking down Vandam Street together."

"Okay," said Ratso dismissively. "So you didn't discover anything?"

"That's not true," said Rambam emphatically. "I *did* discover something."

"What's that?" asked Ratso.

"I think Tom Baker's hosing Kinky's girlfriend."

23

For a guy who had the mind of a modern-day Sherlock Holmes, I figured it was definitely time for me to start using my head for something other than a hat rack. Not that I doubted Rambam's acuity. It wouldn't be the first time in the history of this fickle, dissembling planet that somebody had hosed somebody behind somebody else's back. Frankly, I was a little disappointed in the Bakerman. Just a little disappointed.

On the other hand, why would the Bakerman, a handsome young devil who could have any woman he desired, be so determined to bone his best friend's current pelvic affiliation? Was it merely the perversity of human nature? Had Rambam read more into their behavior than was merited? Was Judy the great long-lost love of my life? Only to that last question did I have an answer and that was of course negatory. The love of my life was already smoke from the Vatican. Smoke from Bergen-Belsen. Smoke from the steam engine on the Canadian-

Pacific. Smoke from the hood of a 1948 Hudson. Smoke from a Benson & Hedges menthol cigarette with the color of blood on a filter the color of snow or cocaine, take your pick. King-size smoke. Smoke that blinds your cowboy heart to everything but the campfires of the past.

That's just what usually happens when you take in a bird with a broken wing, I thought. Once the wing heals good and strong they beat you to death with it. Nevertheless, I'd have to have a little locker-room chat with my good pal the Bakerman. I'd also need to interview my loyal girlfriend Judy. And possibly most important, I had to remember not to let these personal issues sidetrack me from grilling Abbie about what he knew of the identity of the mysterious person who'd caused particles of glass to fly rapidly into the back of my neck. Whether the glass comes from the Sistine Chapel or the window of a hack, the experience is invariably a painful one you do not soon forget. Also, as if I had to remind myself, a good detective always keeps the following credo emblazoned upon his scrotum: "Trust no one." Given the circumstances, that wouldn't be too difficult.

These were my thoughts as I watched Eighth Avenue slide by my window while the yellow taxicab of my flickering faith rattled its weary way toward the home I didn't have. I got out somewhere in the Village and walked the rest of the way. Though I was wearing the black Stetson hat, nobody tried to take a shot at me. Nobody even shouted: "Hi, cowboy!" Maybe I really was losing my sex appeal. Ah well, sex is forever overrated, they say. To that I might add that taking a Nixon is forever underrated.

Darkness and drizzle were crashing the party by the time I

hooked a right on Vandam and headed for the loft. Behind the trash Dumpster I saw a figure lurking about dressed like a garbageman. Rambam, evidently, was already back on the job.

"What do you think?" I said. "Should I dump Judy?"

"You dump her, bud," said the garbageman, "we'll cart her off."

It was not Rambam.

Tom Baker was fastidiously futzing with the percolator as I entered the loft. I shook the rain from my hat, glanced to the empty bedroom, and with some little effort walked over to the kitchen to watch the operation. Baker was delicately placing several small pieces of eggshell into the coffee grounds.

"Three questions," I said.

"Ask away, lad," said Baker. "That's how we learn about life and love and madness and how to put little particles of eggshell into your coffee."

"First," I said. "Where's Abbie?"

"You mean Barry Freed?"

"Let me ask the questions," said I irritably. "Where the hell is he?"

"Gone when I got here. That was about an hour ago. Next?"

"*Why* do you put eggshells in the coffee?"

"It's just something I've been doing for a long, long time. It's a one-man tradition. It may not really make the coffee taste any better, but it does seem to take some of the bitterness out of life. What's the third question?"

"Did you hose Judy last night?"

Tom Baker stood there for a moment like a man having a conversation with his tie. Then he laughed heartily.

"Could you repeat that last question?" he said.

"You heard me," I said, not amused. "Did you plow Judy?"

"Of course not," said Bakerman. "She's pretty impetuous sometimes, but she's a righteous broad. And she's *your* broad and you're *my* pal. She *is* a little more cosmopolitan than you are. We got stoned on some heroin last night at this club. Smack'll do some funny things to you and, frankly, I don't think I could've hosed her last night even with Ratso's penis. She's liberal-minded but loyal and I'd *never* fuck a dame of yours. Now maybe if she was your wife."

"I'm saving myself for Anne Frank," I said.

"We *did* have some fun," said Baker, his green eyes twinkling mischievously. "But all I wound up doing was give her a haircut."

"So now she looks like a French newsboy?"

"No such luck."

"An Oscar Wilde pageboy sort of style?"

"Never touched a hair on her head," said Baker. "As the Brits might say, I just gave her trim a little trim. Hope you don't mind, old boy."

Whether we were still close enough to the free love of the sixties or whether Tom Baker's perennial Irish charm had prevailed, I do not know. I just know it seemed much funnier than it did serious. I also realized that I could never love Judy as much as I loved the Bakerman. Not that I'd soon be walking around the Village wearing a Greek sailor's cap. It was just that I'd never really given Judy a chance. Before I'd met her, death had sold me a paper doll.

By the time Baker poured us both a cup of his gourmet coffee, the tension convention was over. He said it was, no doubt, the heroin talking. The devil made him do it. I was more amused than angry.

"At least," he said, "I always tell you the truth. That's more than you can say for certain other pals of yours. Barry Freed, for instance. When somebody's following you around trying to ice you, you usually have at least some idea of who the fucker is. I think your pal knows something he's not telling you."

"I'll ask him some questions, too."

"Good. Just remember, whatever he hasn't told you almost got you killed last night."

"Mistaken identity."

"You're pretty cavalier about things."

"What things?"

"The crazy bullshit with me and Judy. A bullet narrowly missing you in a taxicab."

"'Between the cradle and the grave,'" I said, quoting Samuel Hoffenstein, "'lies a haircut and a shave.'"

24

I'd known Tom Baker since Christ was a cowboy, but only in the last two or three years had his behavior become worrisomely erratic. This decline in judgment, general stability, and just plain good sense—the latter of which Baker never really had in the first place—I attributed largely to heroin. It's never easy to try to prevent the decline and fall of a dear, heroic friend. It was particularly difficult from my vantage point, which was usually rather high, a situation attributable largely to cocaine. It is a fact of life, and sometimes death, that heroin and cocaine send people to different planets, neither of which, of course, ever happens to be earth. That's the point of it all, I guess. Like Slim, my old friend back in Texas, always says: "You gotta find what you like and let it kill you."

Though the Bakerman incident certainly had the ring of truth, that was hardly my problem now. My personal life, if you still wanted to call it that, would have to take a back seat in the taxicab to my redoubled determination to crack the mystery of who was trying to croak Abbie Hoffman. Ratso had threatened to come the following morning and I was almost looking forward to his visit. As my trusty Dr. Watson, I had to admit, he did lend a certain naïveté to any investigation. Always provided, of course, that there was someone to investigate. By Cinderella time, Abbie had still not returned to the loft.

The Bakerman had gone to a party, so I decided it might be a good time to peruse the worldly possessions Abbie had left in the bedroom. I had no problem with this mild invasion of his privacy. It was my firm conviction that all our lives were at risk until I could shed some light upon the identity of the person who was shadowing him.

For a former hippie, and a former Yippie, the guy was surprisingly neat. This, I reflected, in stark contrast to his previous hostesticle, Ratso, the world's only anal-retentive slob. The other problem with tossing Abbie Hoffman's possessions was that there just weren't a hell of a lot of possessions to toss. Only one partially full duffel bag and most of the contents were clothing.

I don't know what it was I was expecting to find, but whatever it was wasn't there. No notes, letters, diary, calendar, address book. Whatever inventory Abbie Hoffman had he apparently carried almost exclusively between his ears. At the bottom of the duffel bag I found a book of poems called *Run with the Hunted* by Charles Bukowski. Bukowski, I knew, had a reputation for being constantly drunk, constantly in the act of vomiting, and, if Ratso could be believed, a close personal friend of his. Possibly that was why Bukowski spent so much time drinking and vomiting.

As I leafed through the book a note fell to the dusty bedroom floor. Feeling like Nancy Drew, I picked up the note and held it up to the exposed lightbulb hanging from the ceiling. In a handwriting that either belonged to Abbie or a left-handed spider-crab it read: "Call Kunstler re: Rams of God." This was followed by a phone number which I assumed belonged to William Kunstler, the famed radical lawyer who'd defended Abbie along with the rest of the Chicago Seven for trying to torpedo the Democratic Convention of 1968 in that city. The way I saw it, they hadn't been wildly successful. When you start a revolution and you wind up with Nixon, it's time to go back to the drawing board.

I put the book and my fugitive friend's meager belongings back into the duffel bag and I put the note in my pocket. At last, I thought, I had something that might possibly constitute what we in the field of crime prevention like to refer to as a lead. It didn't seem like much, but it might just be the ticket that would keep my cowboy hat from exploding. If Abbie continued to pull his lips together, I'd confront him with the note. If I still didn't get satisfaction, maybe I could get the information out of Kunstler. If you're looking for someone who will sell somebody out, your first stop is a lawyer. I went over to the rickety little table, pulled up the orange crate, and dialed a familiar number on the blower. A familiar rodentlike voice answered.

"Kinkstah!" it said. "I was having a nightmare."

"So was I," I said, "but I wasn't sleeping. Who're the Rams of God?"

"I've heard of them," said Ratso. "They're a born-again professional football team."

"I'm afraid not, my dear Watson," I said. "They could be a vital clue that may help us catch our culprit."

"Catch this," said Ratso. Then, very audibly, he expelled a rather large amount of gas.

After cradling the blower, I lit up a cigar and walked downstairs to see if I could find Rambam. I was convinced I had something with the Rams of God note and I thought maybe Rambam could shed some wool on the subject. The bum was sleeping in the lobby again in his ragged old overcoat and with a black watch cap pulled over his eyes. As I walked past he stirred slightly then turned his body against the wall.

"If this fucking stakeout goes on much longer," he said, "I'm going to run out of identities."

"Rambam," I said. "Just the guy I've been looking for."

"Too bad I can't nab the guy I'm looking for," he said. "I've spotted him a couple of times lurking around in back of the building, but he may be getting wise to me. Also that goddamn cop Cooperman's been giving me grief for loitering."

"Maybe this'll help," I said, handing him the note. "I did a little detecting myself and found it in Barry Freed's duffel bag."

"William Kunstler," said Rambam. "Total scumbag. What's Barry Freed doing calling William Kunstler?"

"Search me."

"I just might," said Rambam suspiciously.

"I'm not sure Kunstler's so important," I said, "but who are the Rams of God?"

"Right-wing religious fanatics," said Rambam. "Sort of a vigilante group."

"Barry received a threatening phone call last night. Somebody said they were going to kill him. Called him a 'Jew bastard.' It could tie in. Right-wing religious fanatics might very well hate Jews."

"There's only one problem," said Rambam.

"What's that?"

"Everybody else does, too," he said.

25

The days flitted by like little yellow butterflies being sucked inexorably into the smiling chrome grillwork of a 1948 Hudson. The man known as Barry Freed did not return to the loft. Ratso began working quite industriously as editor of *High Times* magazine. The Bakerman continued to burn the candle at both its ends, and sometimes I could almost see its ghostly light flickering faintly in his eyes. I'm not sure what happened to Rambam that fateful week. Maybe he was involved with the police academy. Possibly he was back in rabbinical school. All I could say for sure was that the bum sleeping in the lobby of the building was now just a bum sleeping in the lobby of the building.

Judy and I continued to see each other, but something was now a little different between us and both of us knew what that something was. Baker, I felt sure, had mentioned our conversation to Judy, but she didn't lamp to it. For my part I thought it was a pretty good haircut and one night in bed, upon close observation of the matter in question, I told her so.

"I like what you've done with your hair," I said.

"I thought you'd never notice," she said.

"Well, I have been a little distracted lately. There've been times that if Harpo Marx had been down there I wouldn't have noticed."

"I would've," she said. "He's not as verbal."

Most of the time, however, when I wasn't with Judy or egging the Bakerman on as he terrorized the patrons of the Monkey's Paw, I lived a dreary, sparsely furnished life in the dreary, sparsely furnished loft. It was a lonely, rather monastic existence much of the time. My reading material was the Charles Bukowski book, and very soon I began seeing rather unfortunate parallels between the unfortunate life of the poet and my own. Both of us drank a lot. Both of us were experiencing recurring bouts of projectile vomiting. And of course both of us knew Ratso.

It was into this tepid cauldron of emptiness that something strange was quite unexpectedly pitched. I was drinking Jameson's one evening whilst smoking a cigar and reading one of Bukowski's sicker efforts for about the seventh time when the phone rang.

"Start talkin'," I said.

"It's me," said a furtive voice.

"Barry?"

"Yeah."

"You all right?" I knew better than to ask him where he was.

"That bastard's still on my tail."

"That guy really gets around," I said. "We've had a few sightings over here, too. What I don't understand is why he keeps following you around and hasn't croaked you yet?"

"You can ask him next time you see him. I'm coming back tonight."

This, to quote my father, was "exactly what I didn't want to happen." Just when I was getting used to being Charles Bukowski, I suddenly had to be Sherlock Holmes again. On top of it all, Abbie definitely sounded like he was cookin' on another planet.

"Okay," I said. "What time are you getting here?"

"Around twenty-two hundred hours."

"I don't completely understand military time," I said. "Besides, the war is over."

"That's what you think," he said. As always, he hung up, for security reasons, just as I was starting to say maybe it wasn't such a good idea.

I'd planned to meet Tom Baker and a few fellow troublemakers that evening at the Monkey's Paw around eleven o'clock. If twenty-two hundred hours was ten o'clock, as I hoped it was, then I'd have time to interrogate Abbie before I got too monstered to care. So I read a little more Charles Bukowski and drank a little more and pretty soon, sure enough, I vomited. It wasn't an entirely unpleasant experience. Indeed, it reminded me vaguely of what Willie Nelson claimed had been Elvis's last words: "Corn? Did I eat corn?"

As it turned out, Judy dropped over before Abbie did and I told her my friend Barry would be crashing in the loft and I wanted to get him squared away and then Judy and I would drift down to the Paw. That sounded like a plan to Judy, who of course didn't know that Barry was Abbie and very possibly didn't care.

Around ten o'clock a storm blew in and not too much after that Abbie blew in as well. I took one look in his eyes and it became quickly apparent to me that he didn't know that Barry was Abbie either and quite possibly didn't give a damn anymore. If Abbie was really finally losing his grip, it could be mildly troubling, I thought, particularly since half the feds in the country were no doubt more than eager to catch him if he fell.

He'd barely gotten in the door before he reached under his overcoat, pulled out a large handgun of some kind, and began waving it wildly around the loft. This sudden action, coupled with the craziness in his eyes, scared the shit out of Judy and didn't do my nerves a hell of a lot of good either.

"VIVA ZAPATA!" he shouted.

"Uh—Barry—I'm not sure that's really—"

"VIVA CHE!!" shouted Abbie, spinning around into a gunfighter's stance.

"Jesus Christ, Abbie—"

"Who's Abbie?" said Judy, ducking behind the kitchen counter.

"Who *is* Abbie?" said Abbie, now aiming the weapon recklessly at imaginary opponents, two of whom appeared to be Judy and myself.

At last the steam seemed to be going out of him, leaving him looking both ancient and childlike at the same time. Like a dead teenager. I took the gun away from him. It wasn't loaded.

"ALL THOSE FOR FREEDOM FOLLOW ME!" he shouted halfheartedly.

We followed him into the bedroom where I gave him two blue Valiums that Dr. Bock had prescribed for Judy. By the time I turned off the light he was already asleep. I took two blue Valiums myself and then Judy and I headed down the stairs and into the rainwept, redolent New York night. Judy didn't say anything until we'd gotten into the hack for the Monkey's Paw.

"Your friend's kind of sad, isn't he?" she said. "His eyes look so lost and brokenhearted. They don't really look like a crazy man. More like a troubled kid. Who is he anyway?"

"Just one of the guys," I said, "who invented the sixties."

26

The rain had let up a bit by the time the hack had spit us out on Seventh Avenue in front of Village Cigars. We wandered in, and Judy bought some cigarettes and I bought five Hoyo de Monterrey Rothschild cigars English Market Selection. This brand of cigar was short and fat, very similar, indeed, for whatever the reason, to many of the people who smoked them. I wasn't short and I was currently skinny as Jesus, so there had to be some other reason for my growing attachment to these little boogers.

"Do me a favor," I said to Judy.

"Anything," said Judy, "except making love on Ratso's couch again."

"Next time you see Dr. Bock, ask him if there's any Freudian reason why I seem to prefer these big, fat, dark brown kind of cigars. Probably I secretly want to smoke Negro penises or something like that, but I might as well get a professional opinion."

"If I ask him that," said Judy, "he'll know that I'm crazy."

"Don't tell him who I am. Just say you have a friend who's a bit worried about his recent compulsion. Then tell me exactly what he says."

"If you're man enough to take it."

"If I can walk around constantly smoking a large Negro penis, I figure I can take just about anything."

"I'll ask him," she said. "But in the meantime I think you should just keep this little problem to yourself."

"Agreed," I said, as I lit up a cigar on the sidewalk. A large, friendly-looking black man with a beret smiled at me and winked rather suggestively. I did not return the wink.

"By the way," I said, "have you had any more Tim sightings recently?"

"I haven't seen Tim," said Judy, "so I suppose it was all in my mind. Now all I'm seeing is big black men winking at you on the sidewalks."

"That's ridiculous," I said.

Moments later, safely inside the bowels of the Monkey's Paw, we found ourselves in a totally different world from that of the street. The Paw seemed to be gripped with a frenzy of activity that night. The noise level was near deafening, but we could hear one voice carrying clearly above the general hubbub of the crowd. It had a happy, mildly threatening singsong tone to it, and it sounded a bit more familiar than I might've liked. The voice was emanating from somewhere near the bar and it kept repeating the same nursery rhyme chorus over and over again like a drunken diabolical mantra. As we moved up to the bar through the crowd we could hear the carefully enunciated words more precisely.

"Do you know the Bakerman? The Bakerman? The Bakerman? Do you know the Bakerman—"

At this point someone would yell "Shut up!" and the irritating little out-of-place performance would momentarily cease. There would be a small undertone of grumbling around the bar, then the noise level would return to near-deafening. Moments later, like the Sirens calling to Ulysses, like a voice on the wind, the little song would cut through again.

"Do you know the Bakerman? The Bakerman? The Bakerman? Do you know the Bakerman?—"

"Shut the fuck up!"

Momentary silence.

Crowd noise.

Almost back to normal.

Then it would happen again.

"Do you know the Bakerman? The Baker—"

"Shut the fuck *up!*"

Tom Baker was smiling mischievously into his Guinness when we pulled up next to him at the bar. On his other side was McGovern, the large Irish reporter with the large head, and a hell-raising but very charming big guy from New Zealand named Ross Waby. The two of them appeared to be enjoying Tom Baker's a cappella performances. No one else at the bar, however, seemed even remotely amused. This looked especially true for the bartender, a big, humorless, constipated control addict named Fred. Evidently Fred had just given the Bakerman a strong dressing down because, aside from the perpetual mischief in his eyes, his demeanor was not dissimilar to that of a chastened schoolboy.

"Whatever happened to free speech?" shouted McGovern

rhetorically to the big bartender's back. The bartender was now busily futzing with the Jewish piano, sometimes referred to as the cash register. No one at the bar paid any attention to McGovern.

"Only in America," said Ross Waby wistfully.

"Whatever happened to 'The customer's always right?'" shouted McGovern a trifle louder.

No response from anyone. I tried to order a round of drinks, but the bartender appeared to now be assiduously avoiding our little portion of the mahogany.

"You guys are poison," I said. "I can't even order a drink."

"I'll see what I can do," said Baker.

Before anyone could stop him he started loudly singing the little nursery rhyme again. This time the bartender shot right over like a guided missile. He leaned over the bar and put his furious face about four inches from Tom's. I watched with fascination as several large veins vibrated menacingly in his neck. For his part, Tom just took a casual swallow of his Guinness.

"I told you to keep it down," said the bartender grimly. "Now if I hear that stupid song one more time I'm throwing you out of here for good. Eighty-sixing you. I mean it, pal. Now don't let me hear that shit again."

Everyone at the bar was watching this little episode and Baker, properly chastised, stared down into his Guinness. When he looked up again the bartender's face, still trembling with rage, was about thirteen inches away, about the length, I surmised, of the average Negro penis.

It started softly and slowly, almost like a lullaby, but because the bar was suddenly so quiet, you could hear it quite clearly. It was Tom Baker singing under his breath. But this time he sang it as sort of an Irish anthem, not especially to stand up against a bartender but to stand up as a man against fate, against the gods, against the way life is in this world. His eyes no longer reflected mere mischief. They now shone brightly with what might best be described as an earthbound charm and a deathbound glory.

"Do you know the Bakerman?" he sang very softly. Crazy as it was, at that moment I knew for sure why I'd always looked up to him as the spiritual older brother I never had.

What happened next happens every night in bars all over the world, almost always involving people who don't know the Bakerman. Fred the bartender and several hefty cohorts came over the bar at Tom Baker, who was more than ready for them. Judy and I and several other nearby customers were thrown around like poker chips in the ensuing melee. Somebody knocked McGovern on his ass and Baker nailed the bartender with a good right cross. McGovern got back quickly to his feet.

"Whatever happened to 'Keep the customer satisfied'?" he shouted.

"We'd better get our boy out of here," said Ross Waby. "The natives look restless."

At last a raft of bar employees pushed and shoved a raging Bakerman out the door of the establishment. The odds were not good, and Ross, McGovern, and I were doing our best to keep them from lynching Tom and at the same time shielding Judy from the flying fists and the crush of the crowd. At the top of the steps Baker turned for one last taunt at his adversaries, many of whom were cheering at his forced departure.

"I've been fat-armed out of better dives than this," he shouted. "I shall return!"

Baker was laughing like a hero or a madman as the five of us crossed Seventh Avenue and headed back to the loft together. There was a strange look of personal triumph in Baker's eyes and I was gratified that I was crazy enough to understand it and share it with him. We were very much like a small parade returning from a war that had almost been victorious.

By the time we'd gotten to Vandam Street, the village was quiet and the peaceful, almost meditative mood seemed to prevail within us as well. We were just debating whether to ankle it over to The Ear or just go back to the loft and kill the rest of my Jameson's when it happened. A huge explosion ripped across the far end of the street. Smoke and debris were billowing out of the windows from one of the lower floors of a nearby building and I could guess which one it was.

"Holy Moly!" said Baker. "That's our flat!"

"Abbie's sleeping in there!" said Judy, tears suddenly coming to her eyes.

"Abbie?" said McGovern, ever on the alert for breaking news. "Abbie Hoffman?"

I nodded silently as little yellow butterflies flitted out of what once had been the windows of my loft. I stood in front of the building in a state of stunned sadness as the little flames licked the darkness and the thick dark smoke drifted like the devil itself into the night.

Baker got the door to the building open and rushed up the stairs with McGovern and Waby close behind him. Judy was sobbing now, and she and I followed them at a slower pace. Considering the devastating size of the blast, there didn't seem to be any reason to hurry. Anyone in that loft would've been a crispy critter by this time.

"How could anyone do this?" Judy said, as the ubiquitous sounds of sirens filled the night.

"I don't know," I said.

"What does it mean?" she asked.

"It means the sixties are finally over," I said.

27

"Come on in, folks!" shouted a figure I recognized through the smoke as Rambam. "We're roasting a few weenies."

"Hopefully not your own," I said, as Judy and I entered the wreckage of the loft. "What the hell are you doing here anyway?"

"Hey," said Rambam cheerfully, "a stakeout's a stakeout. This time, unfortunately, the bastard gave me the slip."

"I can see that," I said.

Before any further social intercourse could take place, another large human shape loomed into view behind Rambam. It was Tom Baker.

"Did you check the bedroom?" I asked him, not entirely sure I wanted to hear the answer.

"No one's here," said Tom. "Just McGovern and Waby, who keep bumping into each other in the smoke. And, of course, our ace stakeout man, Rambam, here."

Rambam and Baker exchanged what might've been withering glances under other circumstances. When enough smoke gets in your eyes it makes it hard to see, much less wither.

"You mean there's no one in the bedroom?" I said.

"He's gone," said Baker.

"Of *course* he's gone," said Rambam. "He got out the back way while I was watching the front. It's too bad I couldn't have been in two places at the same time. I followed him, but he got away. I guess I'll have to turn in my Captain Midnight magic transporter ring."

"So Abbie's alive!" said Judy, tears coming to her eyes again.

I couldn't tell if her tears were merely from the smoke or from the fact that another dinosaur from the sixties had as yet escaped extinction. In a way, I supposed, it didn't really matter. In another way, maybe it did. You'd like to think yesterday could be a player in tomorrow's game, but often as not everything simply gets rained out.

"Abbie?" said Rambam.

"The guy who's gone is Barry Freed," I said.

"The guy who's gone is going to be me," said Rambam, "and that's going to leave you in a world of shit. Just who is Barry Freed and where did he go?"

"You followed him," said Baker. "You tell us."

"The subject was last seen," said Rambam, "wearing an old army jacket and standing on the fire escape lobbing a hand grenade."

By this time McGovern and Waby had fairly well commandeered whatever was left of the liquor cabinet, Baker was rapidly squirreling away a stash of marching powder, and the cops could be heard heavily clambering up the stairways of the old warehouse. Rambam grabbed me by the arm and led me over to the rear of the loft, where the guy had apparently lobbed the grenade. The damage was heavier here and so was the conversation.

"If I'd known that Barry Freed was Abbie Hoffman," said Rambam evenly, "I might've enjoyed watching him get blown to bits by a grenade."

"But he didn't," I said. "He must've slipped out the front of the building when you were chasing the blond-haired guy in the army jacket around the back."

"Yeah. Too bad. I should've known from your friend's furtive behavior and the little mention about William Kunstler that Barry Freed wasn't who you said he was. Unfortunately, I took you at your word."

"I'm sorry. I just thought that protecting Abbie's identity wherever possible was just about as important as protecting Abbie."

"Protecting yourself from me might become important if you ever ask for my help again under false pretenses. If I'd known that fucker was Abbie Hoffman I'd never have helped you investigate this shit. If I'm going to put my life at risk I want to know why."

"That's what I'm trying to figure out."

"You better start figuring."

"Tell me about the guy you followed. How'd you lose him?"

"It really wasn't very hard. I was on foot and he had a car."

"The four-wheeled penis strikes again."

"There seem to be a lot of penises involved in this operation," said Rambam, as the cops appeared to be finishing up with Tom Baker and heading our way.

"Notice anything about the car? Did you get a license number? Was there anybody with him?"

"Yes, no, and no. It was a late-model Buick. Couldn't get the license number, but I did notice something interesting. The car had Carolina plates. North or South, I couldn't say for sure."

"My money's on North."

"How the hell could you know that?"

"I don't know for sure. But I have a strange premonition that possibly, for the first time in history, the North shall rise again."

"I'll save my subway tokens," said Rambam.

28

The smoke cleared out, so did the cops, and not too long after that, so did the Bakerman and myself. Abbie, of course, had cleared out long before we had, with the exploding grenade ringing in his ears and, quite understandably, paranoia gripping his pilgrim heart. I was no longer quite so certain his paranoia was justified, however. I was going back over what we knew and what we didn't know and the patterns seemed to be shifting ever so slightly in my mind. I had a lot of opportunity to carefully analyze the situation. Now that the second-floor loft on Vandam Street was rendered unlivable, surely breaking the landlord's little heart, I had relocated back where I'd started from. At least now I had the good services of my faithful Dr. Watson to help me along with what I perceived to be a singularly dangerous phase of the investigation.

"If you don't like the fucking couch," said Ratso, "you can sleep on the fucking floor."

"I'm afraid the Virgin Mary might fall down in the night," I said, "and crush me to death."

"Well, at least nobody's heard from Abbie lately. He seems to be the source of all the trouble."

"I'm not so sure of that anymore."

"What do you mean, Kinkstah? Everything started the day Abbie came over here to the apartment. Don't you agree?"

"If I told you what I really thought, Watson, I doubt very much if you'd believe me."

"Try me."

"Sexually?"

"No," said Ratso irritably, "just tell me your theory, Sherlock."

"My theory is: When you're dealing with a case of mistaken identity it's never best foot forward to be mistaken."

"Come again?"

"Sexually?"

"That's about the worst theory I've heard since Hanoi getting bombed would terminate the war."

"Maybe us getting bombed might terminate this discussion."

"Seriously, Kinkstah. *Who* was mistaken about mistaken identity? What the hell are you yapping about?"

"Well, it's a crazy idea and I don't know where it gets us, but it has been starting to get up my sleeve a bit lately. Who was here with Abbie when he first claimed there was a guy down in the street following him?"

"You and me."

"Correct, Watson. You don't miss much, do you?"

"Just most of my life. Go ahead."

"Who was in the taxi when a bullet almost took my head off a few weeks ago?"

"You were alone, you said."

"That's right. Just me and the driver."

"So who was driving the taxi? Harry Chapin?"

"Your mind is working Watson, but unfortunately you're missing the point entirely. Remember when Abbie wore the black cowboy hat the night before and claimed somebody'd shot at him? What if the shooter didn't mistake me for Abbie? What if he mistook Abbie for me?"

"Great idea, Sherlock, but Professor Moriarty hasn't been seen around these parts lately. With all respect, who'd want to whack you?"

"Whose phone did the threatening 'Jew bastard' call come in on?"

"Yours."

"Whose loft did somebody toss a hand grenade into last week?"

"Yours, but—"

"We must be careful, Watson. Very careful."

Here Ratso stood up suddenly and began walking quickly back and forth between the Virgin Mary and the half-eaten pastrami sandwich sitting on the counter. Every once in a while he'd stop to take a bite. Every once in a while I'd stop to snort a line of marching powder off Ratso's framed photo of Elvis meeting Nixon.

"How much cocaine are you doing?" he asked at last.

"Just enough to keep me from falling asleep on this couch."

"Well, aside from being paranoid, ridiculous, and fanciful—"

"I knew you'd see things my way—"

"—your theory overlooks the most elementary element of any criminal investigation. Motive! Who would bother to try to kill a broke-dick, coke-addicted, over-the-hill Jewish country singer from Texas—"

"Don't put me up on a pedestal now—"

"—who's currently crashing on my couch?"

"My coke dealer?"

"Your coke dealer is the last one to want you dead. What would happen to all his profits?"

"*Her* profits."

"But it always comes back to motive. Motive! Motive! Motive! *Lots* of people might want Abbie Hoffman dead. *Nobody* wants you dead, Kinkstah."

I lay back on the couch and stared, glassy-eyed, at the glassy eyes in the polar bear's head. My own head felt stuffed with ice. The stuff of dreams was far away from me now. Somewhere with Abbie Hoffman. With Kacey. With lovers and ghosts who gave a damn. For a moment I saw my reflection in the deep, cold river of the polar bear's eyes, where Phil Ochs and Michael Bloomfield fished forever among the stars. Ratso had been right, of course. Nobody wanted me dead. Nobody had any motive. Except, very possibly, myself.

Somehow I nodded off, grinding my teeth and counting Ratsos in red pajamas eating pastrami sandwiches. After a fitful four-hour power nap I woke up not only somewhat pleased to still be alive but, more important, knowing what had to be done. It's amazing what a good night's sleep will do for you.

I rushed to the bedroom, woke up Ratso, and told him my

plan. He seemed very excited about the new direction of my thinking.

"William Kunstler!" he ejaculated. "I *know* William Kunstler. He's a personal *friend* of mine."

"Let's hope he feels the same way," I said.

29

Being a private dick is really pretty simple. Once you run out of cocaine, crazy ideas, and self-pitying bullshit, you're eventually left with the truth. The truth was that Abbie, probably very wisely, had gotten the hell out of Dodge, and Rambam, the one guy who might be pissed off enough to have a motive to kill, had driven off in a 1937 Snit. It wasn't likely, I figured, that I'd be seeing either of these key players any time soon. All I really had going for me was the ever-loyal, ever-tedious Ratso, and one lousy little note of Abbie's about William Kunstler and the Rams of God. As Abbie's longtime lawyer and the attorney for the Chicago Seven, if anyone could help us it would be Kunstler. Had there been threats and murder attempts against Abbie before? Were the Rams of God involved? Was there merely a pattern of paranoia here? Was Kunstler even still in touch with Abbie? Only when I had the answers to these questions could I know whether or not there was any merit to the cocaine-induced nightmare of a lone gunman in an army jacket lurking somewhere in New York City and aiming—not too accurately, thank the Baby Jesus—to kill the Kinkster.

Sherlock Holmes, who had a few cocaine-induced nightmares himself, always believed very strongly in stripping away the impossible. Once you accomplished that, he thought, you'd be left with the one thing mankind has consistently rejected, maligned, and almost totally ignored down through the ages, the truth. Frankly, I wasn't sure that I wanted to know it myself. But I couldn't dance and I didn't have any hobbies, so I figured I might as well find out. It's possibly worth noting that beginning with Moses and Jesus and Socrates and Copernicus and Galileo and Columbus right on down to Martha Mitchell, the Cassandra of Watergate, something terrible has always happened to anyone who through perseverance or mere fate has stumbled upon the truth. When your current zip code is Ratso's couch, of course, terrible might be a good career move.

"No, it's *Ratso,*" Ratso was saying to somebody in Kunstler's office. "Of course I can spell it. R-A-T-S-O! Just tell Bill it's Ratso. He'll know me."

It didn't sound like a really auspicious beginning, so I wandered away from Ratso's little rathole of an office into the living room and lit up a cigar. Ratso was still operating at a fairly loud decibel level, and it was a rather painful thing to hear his end of the conversation.

"Whatta ya mean 'Ratso is not known to him'? I met him at the Chicago Convention. We were out on the street. I was standing right between Jerry Rubin and the Tibetan monk. He said to call him when I was back in New York . . . Ratso . . . R-A-T-S-O . . ."

I was only half-listening to Ratso now. I looked at the Virgin Mary's face and she looked at mine. Her plaster eyes seemed inescapably sad. I'm not sure what my eyes might've revealed. You'd have to ask the Virgin Mary.

"Fucking lawyers," Ratso said moments later as he walked desultorily into the room. "Can you imagine that guy?"

"May all his juries be well hung," I said. "Get his address, Watson. We may be paying him a little uninvited visit."

With all due haste, possibly in an effort to cover his wounded pride, Ratso quickly came up with the street address of Kunstler's law firm. For once, fate was on our side. I'd seen the address of that building before and it didn't take me long to remember where I'd seen it. My old friend from the University of Texas, Chinga Chavin, had recently opened his first advertising business in the very same building. Chinga had formed a band roughly around the time I'd put together the Texas Jewboys. He called the group Country Porn and, though Chinga had what I liked to call "negative stage charisma," they achieved a fair modicum of success for a while around the country. Chinga also could pen a pretty good country song now and then. My personal favorite of his was always "Cum Stains on the Pillow (Where Your Sweet Head Used to Be)."

While Chinga may have had the heart of a poet, he had the brain of a scammer, which not only accounted for his success in advertising but also explained my confidence in his participation in the furtive little scheme I had in mind. With Chinga's help I felt sure we could get onto Kunstler's floor after the building had closed, but that alone would not be enough. It would be comparable perhaps to God allowing Moses only to see the Promised Land but not allowing him to enter. After forty years of wandering in the desert, I wasn't about to let God or anybody else keep me from getting my hands on Abbie Hoffman's confidential legal files.

The only thing missing from the operation was a way to get into the law office itself, and the only guy I knew who might be able to do it was Rambam, and the only problem was that at the moment he had definitely taken somewhat of a scunner to the Kinkster. I had to somehow get him back on my side and it had to be soon. Living on Ratso's couch was bad enough, but not knowing whether a psycho killer is gunning for Abbie Hoffman or for you yourself is not a situation recommended for improving your mental hygiene.

"So what's the plan, Sherlock?" asked Ratso, sometime later while taking a short break from watching hockey and eating a Big Wong's to-go order of roast pork and scrambled eggs over rice.

"Our little raiding party goes into action tonight, Watson. We meet Chinga and Rambam in front of the building at midnight."

"How'd you get Rambam back on board?"

"I told him my own life might be in danger."

"It's certainly possible," said Ratso. "You might take too much cocaine some night and fall off the couch."

"I also appealed to his sense of Jewish honor."

"Say what?"

"He *is* in rabbinical school."

"How the hell is *that* going to help?"

"Well, let's just say he also seems to be pretty well-versed in several fields of nonrabbinical study."

"So let me get this straight, Sherlock. It's you, me, your friend Chinga, and Rambam all breaking into William Kunstler's law offices tonight at midnight?"

"That's correct, Watson."

"Great!" he shouted, literally jumping for joy. "A Jewish Watergate!"

"Watson," I said, "you always cease to amaze me."

30

One of the mild little ironies of crime solving, not to mention life, is that if you want to be a good guy you've got to be able to think like a bad guy. There's never existed a good little church-worker with the God-given talent to casually crawl inside the criminal mind. God gives good little church-workers other things: grief, guilt, absolution, moral superiority, blissful ignorance, the ability to see the world the way it never was and never will be. If all of this fails to add up to any semblance of true happiness, it's not really surprising. That's why when you look back over the fleeting yet inescapably tedious history of mankind, you'll always find more criminals than church-workers.

With these bright but spiritually vexing thoughts in mind, I stood on a midtown Manhattan sidewalk at midnight, smoking a cigar and listening to Rambam and Ratso's idle chatter.

"What the fuck are we waiting for?" said Rambam. With

his coat, tie, and attaché case he looked like a dapper young executive sixteen hours late for work.

"With your vast rabbinical training," said Ratso, "we're waiting for you to bless this little venture."

"You'll be waiting a long time," said Rambam.

"Tell me, Kinkstah," said Ratso, "is there really a Chinga? My little friends tell me he doesn't exist."

"You don't have any little friends," I said.

"He doesn't have any big ones either," said Rambam.

"If I did have any," said Ratso, oblivious to any form of insult, "I doubt if they'd be leaving my ass waiting here on the sidewalk at midnight."

"Chinga's always late," I said. "It's the only consistent trait he's got."

As we continued to wait for Chinga Chavin, Rambam walked over and cased the front of the building, Ratso walked the other way and cased the front window of a closed gourmet deli, and I continued to smoke the cigar and ponder life as I thought I knew it. The more I pondered, the more paranoid I became. Being a private dick, I reflected, could be hazardous to your health, not to mention your dick.

After what seemed like the gestation period of the southern sperm whale, Chinga turned up in a high state of nervous energy and the four of us held a brief caucus on a corner out of sight of the building's entrance. I introduced Chinga to Ratso and Rambam. None of the three of them seemed to be even remotely bonding with one another. This was fine with me. We weren't networking; we were breaking and entering.

"I can get you into the gates of the city," said Chinga. "You guys'll have to do the rest."

"No problem," said Rambam.

"By the way, Sherlock," said Ratso, "what exactly are we looking for? Directions through the woods to Abbie's house?"

"We're not trying to find Abbie—"

"That's good," said Rambam.

"We're trying to find the truth about Abbie," I said somewhat cryptically. I had to be somewhat cryptic. It was about all I had in stock.

"Okay," said Chinga eagerly. "Let's go. Lock pinkies!"

In a rather remarkable display for an adult, Chinga then proceeded to curl the little finger of his right hand tightly around the little finger of my left hand. He extended his other little finger to Rambam and then to Ratso, but they demurred.

"Locking pinkies is something Kinky and I used to do in college for good luck," said Chinga.

"It doesn't seem to have brought you any," said Ratso.

"There's no sure way to tell," said Chinga. "We don't know what would've happened if we'd never locked pinkies."

"I can't believe I'm seeing this," said Rambam. "Two supposedly grown, supposedly heterosexual men, locking pinkies after midnight out on the street just moments before they may be busted on a class-one felony."

"That's why we're locking pinkies," said Chinga.

"Looks like you've already locked pinkies with a lawnmower," said Ratso, combining the power of keen observation of detail with that of blunt, thoughtless articulation, a process that usually occurs only as standard equipment in a young child.

Indeed, it was true that Chinga had Band-Aids around the

lower knuckles of three fingers and a thumb, not to mention a small, square Band-Aid plastered to his face just below his right temple. The wounds were self-inflicted, caused by the fingernails of the other hand. Clearly, I felt, this behavior was the result of Chinga's having a brilliant pharmacist. Frankly, just at the moment, I wanted two of whatever he was on.

"My shrink contends," said Chinga, "that these injuries are the result of a grooming mechanism gone awry."

"That's fascinating," said Rambam, as he herded the three of us toward the building and patted his attaché case almost lovingly. "Let's just hope the mechanism in *here* doesn't go awry."

"What you got in there?" asked Ratso.

"A plastic inflatable Trojan horse," said Rambam. "Just in case the Missing Link here can't get us into the gates of the city."

"Now remember," I said, as we followed Chinga up to the entrance of the building, "we're three of Chinga's executives burning the midnight oil on a vitally important advertising campaign. So look like executives."

"Impossible for you and Ratso," said Rambam.

"Okay," I said, "so we'll *act* like executives."

"How do we act like executives, Kinkstah?" asked Ratso, as he adjusted his coonskin cap.

"Just act terribly preoccupied, mildly bored, and don't spit on the sidewalk."

Then Chinga put a card in a slot, buzzed a door open, and led us into the foyer. We followed him like three lost little ducklings, across miles and miles of bathroom tiles, toward the security desk. A large man in a rent-a-cop outfit was already giving us the fish-eye.

"All those for fornication follow me," said Chinga.

We did and, in a manner of speaking, that's exactly what happened to us.

31

"Thanks, Chinga," said Rambam rather definitively as we entered the ninth-floor lobby of his advertising agency. "That was a swell elevator ride."

"Wait a fucking minute," said Chinga. "I'm part of this operation. I'm going with you guys down to Kunstler's office. You wouldn't even be here without me."

"Great," said Rambam. "That's all we need. We've already got Hopalong Cassidy and Davy Crockett here and now we've got another Jewish meatball to tag along. I'm telling all you amateur sleuths right now, if we're nabbed in the act tonight it's a class-one felony."

"What'll they give us for this?" asked Chinga, taking out a large bindle of white powder and rolling up a twenty-dollar bill into a straw.

"Jesus Christ," said Rambam, as Ratso helped himself to an audible snort of marching powder, "Kinky, do you know this guy?"

"I'll let you know in a minute," I said, as Ratso passed me the straw and I proceeded to blow away half of my left nostril.

"Look," said Rambam in disgust, "I'm the guy who's going to be breaking and entering into Kunstler's office. I'm not going to put my ass on the line for a bunch of cokeheads."

"Wouldn't look good on the ol' rabbinical résumé," said Ratso.

"It also wouldn't look very good if I ripped your heart out," said Rambam.

"Now, girls," said Chinga, "let's all work together for the t-e-a-m."

"F-u-c-k y-o-u," said Rambam.

The little group bantered on good-naturedly in this fashion for a while longer, then proceeded with the battle plan. Our goal was to come out of the experience alive with Abbie Hoffman's legal files. The first step was for Chinga to take us down two floors' worth on a little-used back stairwell to William Kunstler's offices. Things began smoothly enough.

"When I walk out of this building," said Rambam, "I never want to see your friend Chinga again."

"I don't want to see me again either," said Chinga. "I have very low self-esteem."

"This place is spooky," said Ratso. "It looks like the fucking catacombs."

"At least there're no security cameras," I said.

"Look at all these paint cans and brushes covered with cobwebs," said Ratso. "When was the last time anybody was down here?"

"I don't know," said Chinga. "I think some faggot named Michelangelo was doing a little work last fall."

"I know an Italian heterosexual who's going to be doing a little work right now," said Rambam, setting down his attaché case and studying the lock on Kunstler's back door.

"Italian?" asked Ratso. "What's an Italian doing in rabbinical school?

"*Half*-Italian," said Rambam, extracting a strange-looking lock-picking device from the briefcase.

"Which half?" piped up Chinga.

"The half that's going to kick you in the ass once I get this door open," said Rambam.

Fortunately for Chinga, perhaps, Rambam did not get the door open all that quickly. In fact there was plenty of time for him to pull out the packet of Irving Berlin's White Christmas on the stairwell several times and pass it around to Ratso and myself behind Rambam's busy back. By that time, Ratso, Chinga, and myself were so high we were starting to get lonely, and the door to Kunstler's offices still appeared to remain inviolate.

"What's taking so long?" said Ratso. "I'm getting damp out here without my rubbers."

Rambam shot Ratso a withering glance and took a fully loaded key ring out of his case. It did seem to be taking quite a long time.

"Couldn't you've brought someone along besides these two stooges?" said Rambam. "A big, husky guy like Tom Baker might've come in handy in case I have to huff and puff and blow this fucking door down."

"The Bakerman's busy," said Ratso. "He's out hosing Kinky's girlfriend."

"All in the past," I said, trying to keep cool about things. "All in the past."

Indeed, as I thought it all over for a moment, the solution to this whole chain of rather troubling, not to say dangerous, events, no doubt lay somewhere in the past. Whether the intended target proved to be Abbie or someone else, it might require a course in history to clear up the mystery. And if we didn't get to the bottom of things, Abbie or someone else was soon going to have his piece taken off the board. Unfortunately, it didn't require a lot of imagination to figure out who the someone else was.

"This may be a little bit sloppier job than I'd thought," said Rambam.

The next thing I heard was a loud cracking noise as Rambam's shoulder hit the door at full tilt, splintering the wood like matchsticks.

"It's not the most subtle break-in," said Chinga admiringly, "but it'll do."

"All right," said Rambam. "Kinky and I will go in and try to find Hoffman's file. You two guys go back upstairs and get the paint. Splash a few drug-crazed hippie slogans on the walls to throw the trail off. Shouldn't be too much of a stretch for you guys. Anything to keep the four of us from winding up in the same holding cell."

When Rambam and I got inside we found, not to our great surprise, that the filing cabinets were also locked. Rambam went to work again and this time had better luck. No alarms had gone off and no security teams had come rushing onto the scene, so we figured the B & E gods must've been smiling on us. It required a bit of secretarial work, but we eventually found Abbie's file, which was thick enough to choke an iguana, and secured it safely inside Rambam's attaché case.

As we slipped out the shattered door we saw that Ratso and Chinga had indeed been hard at work. In bright red paint they'd written "Helter-Skelter," "Kill the pigs," "Remember Che," and several other slogans on the wall. Rambam and I studied their handiwork for a moment as Ratso and Chinga stood by proudly, brushes in hand, like modern incarnations of Tom Sawyer and Huck Finn.

"Very convincing," said Rambam rather grudgingly. "Next time we need drug-crazed hippies, we'll give you a call."

"Yeah," I said. "I especially like 'Help! I'm trapped inside William Kunstler's law offices.'"

"That was *my* idea," said Chinga brightly. "I also did 'Say it out loud! I'm Black and I'm proud!'"

"Nobody mentioned 'Wayne Newton is God,'" said Ratso. "What do you think of 'Wayne Newton is God'?"

"Weak," I said.

"It's not true, either," said Chinga. "Everybody knows that Rambam is God."

32

We took the back stairwell up two floors to Chinga's lobby, then grabbed an Otis box down to the main floor. If the B & E itself wasn't too smooth, at least we could make our exit look good. We chatted idly in the self-contained fashion of executives who believed that leaving a building correctly is important spiritual etiquette. That's about the only spiritual thing executives ever do and they'll die trying to get it right.

"Good job, Jennings," said Chinga to Ratso, with a patronizing little clap on the shoulder. "Your work on the Funknuts Account should get you an advance in the company."

"That's great to hear, J.B.," said Ratso. "But right now I'm going home to spank my monkey."

"Very sensible," said Chinga. "You've worked hard, now it's time to free the hostages."

"Unfortunately, J.B.," said Ratso, "I've been masturbating about eight times a day."

"That *is* a bit excessive," said Chinga, tossing a jaunty little salute to the security guy who was severely on the nod and obviously didn't know or care who the hell Chinga was.

We made it out the front doors without being intercepted by a SWAT team. In fact, the only guy who seemed to pay us any attention at all was a bum on the street who wanted money for the United Negro Pastrami Fund. Like a good little executive, I gave him a few bucks. Then we all said our good-byes in front of the building.

"Rambam and I still have to go over these files," I said, "but on behalf of the United Negro Pastrami Fund I want to thank all of you for your help tonight. Needless to say, not a word of our charming little adventure is ever to be mentioned to anyone until we all wake up in hell next to Spiro Agnew."

"I was hoping for Oscar Wilde," said Chinga.

"I was hoping," said Rambam with some force, "that you'd understand that this is serious. Especially *you,* Chinga. I want to be goddamn sure you grasp the gravity of the situation."

"Lock pinkies?" asked Chinga.

Rambam looked on in potentially dangerous disbelief.

"Four-man locked pinkies?" Chinga persisted, extending both little fingers and wiggling them invitingly.

"Let's get out of here," said Rambam.

I gave Chinga a brief locked pinkie for old times' sake, then followed Rambam up the street, with Ratso stringing along.

"Will I see you later, Watson?" I asked.

"Sure, Sherlock," he said. "I really am going home to spank my monkey."

"What a surprise," said Rambam over his shoulder.

"Remind me not to lock pinkies with you," I said.

It was sometime later at a quiet corner table at Sarge's Deli on Third Avenue that Rambam and I were finally able to delve freely into the mysterious fugitive life of my friend Abbie Hoffman. Everything was here. At least everything we needed to draw some rather sobering conclusions about the matter.

"The Rams of God are out of it," said Rambam, eating a pickle. "They're a southern-based right-wing group of wing nuts who totally self-destructed over ten years ago."

"Possibly, they only exist today in Abbie Hoffman's paranoid brain," I offered, as I offered Rambam another pickle. "After all he was down South with the Freedom Riders in the early sixties. You can't blame a guy who's been through what he's been through for thinking someone's after him."

"Hell no," said Rambam. "That's exactly how they nailed Dillinger coming out of the movies. When you've been a federal fugitive for years, on the run and living from place to place underground, you'd be crazy not to go crazy. You let up for one minute and they zap your ass. Abbie's probably got more imaginary demons after him than Linda Blair."

"And, of course, it's very likely that there's no one really after him."

"More than very likely. Look at the reports from the psychologist Kunstler sent him to. This guy says Abbie's 'at times totally out of touch with reality . . . delusionary . . . displays classic paranoid behavioral patterns. . . .' Of course, in New York, that doesn't help us much."

"In other words, the psychologist thought Abbie was cookin' on another planet—"

"No question about it. Take a look for yourself."

I scanned the psychological profiles for a moment or two

and then, in the manner of a Jewish Cadillac, something made me stop on a dime and pick it up.

"Hold the weddin'," I said. "I don't believe this."

"Why not? It's very natural to start imagining things when you've been on the run for a long time. If you and I were fugitives—"

"Hold the back pages," I said. "I'm not talking about Abbie's mental hygiene. It's the shrink or psychologist or whatever the hell he is. Dr. Richard Bock."

"What about him? If he's like most shrinks, he's probably crazier than Abbie, you, me, and Chinga put together. Shrinks are very sick people—"

"He's the same guy that Judy's seeing."

"Judy's definitely cookin' on another planet and she's definitely seeing a number of guys. What's so strange about that?"

"Maybe I'm just looking for something that isn't here, but there's ninety-seven million shrinks and psychologists in New York City and you're telling me it's not unusual that the same one treated both Judy and Abbie?"

"Maybe this psychologist is the guy in the army jacket who thought he was on Iwo Jima last week and lobbed a pineapple into your loft."

"Maybe our waiter's Heinrich Himmler."

"What *is* strange," said Rambam, helping himself to a matzoh ball from my soup, "is that Judy comes from North Carolina, so you say, and the guy I chased definitely had Carolina license plates."

"Maybe our waiter's Orville Wright."

"What's worrisome about all this shit in the files is not only the psychological crap about Hoffman, but it's Kunstler's hard-and-fast, long-held opinion that there's absolutely no-body pursuing Abbie. Kunstler's his lawyer, he's known Abbie forever, and he makes it pretty clear that Abbie's just like the rest of us poor bastards. He wants to be wanted. Unfortunately for Abbie, as time goes by, people care less and less, and your friend turns into a relic of the past."

"An insect trapped in amber."

"That's exactly right."

"I was referring to something in my soup."

Rambam straightened out the files and put them back into his briefcase. His Italian-Jewish blue-green eyes looked at me with a cold, rather foreboding glint.

"Listen to me carefully," he said. "All these files tell us is what we already should've known. Kunstler's saying that his client has pulled this shit many times before and there's absolutely nothing to it. This crazy stalker out there is very real, you see. The only problem is, he's not after Abbie."

I felt a sudden lump in my throat, and it wasn't a matzoh ball. Rambam was getting very close to my own current line of thinking and I damn sure didn't want to find out that I'd been right.

"I told Ratso this same idea recently and he said it was a paranoid cocaine-induced nightmare and I should forget about it."

"Ratso's a fucking idiot."

"I'll mention that to him."

"Be my guest. I've suspected this actually for a long time. Since that night at the Lone Star up on the roof with you, Baker, and the giant iguana, who probably has more common sense than either of you. You wanted me to stake out your place to protect a friend of yours, Barry Freed, who, of course, you didn't mention was Abbie Hoffman."

"A minor detail."

"You're right. Because it sounded to me, even then, like the guy who goes to the doctor and says 'I've got a sick friend'—"

"And the doctor says: 'Okay, pull him out and let's take a look at him.'"

"Not quite," said Rambam, not quite smiling. "The doctor knows you're talking about yourself."

"Mother of God," I said. "You mean you've suspected the guy's been after me the whole time?"

"Why in hell do you think I stayed so long on that freezing, godforsaken stakeout?"

"And all this time I thought it was because you wanted to be a garbageman when you grew up."

"If that were the case," said Rambam, "I'd've been a lawyer."

33

The view from Ratso's couch was still fairly hideous, but, for the first time, I was beginning to see a few other things that were, if possible, even more disquieting. There was a madman loose in New York City who very likely would've croaked me by now if he hadn't on several occasions confused me with my ubiquitous housepest, Abbie Hoffman. Not only, in my opinion, had the hand grenade been meant for me, as well as the potshots taken at Abbie in the black cowboy hat, but the scurrilous "Jew bastard" threatening phone call had also most probably been somebody trying to reach out and touch the Kinkster. The caller may well have thought that Abbie was me. People who're looking to intimidate someone in such a way usually don't take the time to distinguish one Jew bastard from another.

Knowing the world-beating, rancorous lifestyle Abbie had lived, it was easy to see him as a target of some crazed killer. Yet, in my heart I knew Rambam's instincts had been more on target than the mysterious stalker had been to date. If Abbie had gone away, maybe the menacing figure in the old army coat would go away, too. It was wishful thinking, of course, but wishful thinking was better than no thinking at all. If I didn't figure out why this vengeful pursuer was on my tail, Ratso's apartment might add a stuffed Kinky head to its already quite eccentric ambience.

"Why would this guy want you to be worm-bait?" Tom Baker rather rhetorically asked one gray afternoon a couple of days later.

"I'm fucked if I know," I said, quite honestly.

"You're fucked either way," said Baker. "But you can't just lay around on this disgusting davenport with skid marks all over it and wait for him to find you. You've got to figure out *why* he's after *you.*"

"*If* he's after you," said Ratso.

"Of course he's after Pinky, I mean Stinky, I mean Dinky, I mean Kinky. There's either something you've done that you're not thinking of, or there's something you've done you're not telling us."

"There's lots of things I've done I'm not telling you."

"There you are," said Baker triumphantly to Ratso. "I even told you that I'd once shaved your girlfriend's woo-woo. That's how straight-up a guy I am."

"Straight up is right," I said.

"You once shaved Kinky's girlfriend's woo-woo?" asked Ratso. "What was it like?"

"Like nothing you've ever seen," said Baker.

"I've seen it right here on this couch," said Ratso. "I've just never shaved it."

"What is all this talk getting us?" I asked at last, filled with a gnawing sense of frustration.

"Horny," said Ratso.

By the time the Bakerman suggested the idea of hiring a number of "Kinky impersonators" to walk up and down Vandam and Prince Streets in order to draw out the perpetrator, I'd pretty much run out of charm. It was a nice, brisk afternoon and, on a solo flight, I departed Ratso's somewhat stultifying environment and drifted rather restlessly from SoHo over to the West Village. I crossed through Sheridan Square and took a quick peek into the window of the Monkey's Paw. Normally, I wouldn't have darkened the door of the Paw until a cold day in Jerusalem, but the place didn't look crowded and the daytime bartender, a good-natured, friendly sort named Tommy, was working the mahogany. I don't know if you'd call Tommy a friend. Bartenders don't usually have too many real friends. Neither, of course, do private investigators. I descended into the place, sat down at the bar, and ordered a Guinness. So far, so good.

"That Guinness has a better head on it than most people I know," I said as Tommy meticulously drew the drink.

"Tom Baker, troublemaker," said Tommy, smiling and shaking his head almost wistfully.

"Some people never learn," I said. "Let me amend that. No people ever learn."

"He's a fool, God bless him," said Tommy.

"We did have a little tension convention in here the other night," I said. "That bartender was a pretty humorless, constipated sort of guy."

"So's the boss," said Tommy. "I'm not even supposed to be

serving you guys. But what the hell. Just watch out for the company you keep."

"Always good advice."

"Speaking of which, there was a guy in here looking for you some time ago. I haven't seen you so I didn't get to tell you. Said he was an old army buddy or something."

"I was in the Peace Corps."

"Maybe that was it. Maybe he just looked like an old army buddy. Wore an old army jacket anyways. Wanted to know what you were doing these days."

"Christ," I said, "I hope you didn't tell him."

"I think I told him you'd become the world's first Texas-Jewish country singer and you played quite a bit over at the Lone Star. He said he'd try to catch your act."

"That's what I'm afraid of. What'd this guy look like?"

"Now that you mention it, he wasn't precisely a savory character. Long, dirty-blond hair. Cold blue eyes. Looked a bit shell-shocked, if you know what I mean. Of course, that could describe most of the customers we get in here."

"Did he ever give his name?"

"John."

I finished the Guinness, and it seemed to settle my nerves a bit. This was the guy, all right, and the time frame fit the picture, too. It was a funny thing to be tracking a guy who at the same time was tracking you, but it no doubt happens more than you think. That's probably why nobody ever finds anybody.

"If this guy comes back," said Tommy, "do you want me to give him any message?"

"Yeah," I said. "Ask him if he's sorry he missed me."

34

A trail may be old and a trail may be cold, but any trail at all beats wandering around this Grand Central Station of a world with a busted valise searching for someone who's never there. As I ankled it over to the Lone Star Cafe, I thought of the three Peace Corps buddies I'd known named John. Not that I thought this guy was one of them, but a good detective never likes to go off half-cocked. I hadn't seen two of my former mates in almost ten years, but we did keep in touch and none of them would know to come to New York and pry details about me out of a bartender at the Monkey's Paw. Just to be certain, I went over the three of them again in my mind as I hooked a left onto Fifth Avenue. John Mapes was a dark-haired guy with brown eyes living in Hawaii. John Schwartz was a dark-haired guy with brown eyes living in Australia. John Morgan had light brown hair and sort of brown-green eyes and was living in Columbus, Ohio. I'd visited him several years back in that depraved, all-American city, and unless he'd dyed his hair, worn blue contact lenses, and joined the Vienna Boys Choir, there was no reason to think he'd be hanging around the Village worming out information about me when I knew he could just pick up the blower. Clearly, this John was no friend of the Kinkster's.

The Lone Star was preparing for a big night with the great Ray Benson, the world's tallest living Jew, and his band, Asleep at the Wheel, performing in a few hours' time. Asleep at the Wheel was about an eleven-piece band and it was going to be interesting to see how they all planned to squeeze onto the stage of the Lone Star, which was about the size of the Rosebud sled in *Citizen Kane.* It would also be interesting to see if I could squeeze any information out of Cleve and Bill Dick about this particular John, who'd almost certainly made the Lone Star his second stop after the Monkey's Paw. Maybe I was on the wrong road, but it could be hazardous to my health if I pulled over to the side now. Somebody might catch *me* asleep at the wheel.

Bill Dick wasn't in, but Cleve was holding the fort. When I walked into the downstairs office he was doing a line off Bill Dick's desk.

"Want a bump?" he asked.

"Yeah," I said, "but first I need some information."

"Christ," said Cleve, "it must be important."

"Has there been some weird guy coming around here looking for me?"

"Every day," said Cleve. "They're called your fans. No broads. Only guys. Very weird."

"I mean one specific guy. Long, dirty-blond hair, blue eyes, wears an old army jacket. Says his name is John. Seen anybody like that?"

"As a matter of fact, I have. He said he was an old friend of yours but had lost contact with you. Wanted to know where you were crashing. I said I thought you were staying at Ratso's pad on Prince Street. He said he knew the place. Why is this important?"

"It's not important," I said. "It's only life or death. I've got to warn Ratso."

"You'd better warn yourself first," said Cleve. "About twenty minutes ago the guy was still sitting at the upstairs bar."

"I think I'll have that line now," I said.

I filled my left nostril, then filled Cleve in on as much as he needed to know about the suspect. Warily, the two of us weaved our way up the darkened basement stairs of the Lone Star, eventually arriving at the midway point of the stairway leading to the upstairs bar.

"I hope this isn't the stairway to heaven," said Cleve.

"I doubt it," I said. "As close as I've come to that was urinating backstage at a Led Zep concert next to Jimmy Page."

"You're going to be urinating next to me if this bird pulls a gun on us."

"The guy's not even here," I said, as we surveyed the upstairs bar, which was totally devoid of clientele.

Cleve checked with the bartender, who thought the guy had left but wasn't sure. The bartender hadn't talked much to the guy. All the guy had wanted to know was when Kinky Friedman was playing the club again.

"Let's just check the roof," I said. "Then I'll call Ratso and tell him to stay indoors, like Emily Dickinson."

"And don't listen to any flies buzzing," said Cleve.

"I'm sure he's gone," I said, as we carefully climbed the back stairs up to the roof where the dressing rooms, dumpers, and the iguana resided. "Any security working the place yet?"

"You're looking at it," said Cleve.

"That's what I was afraid of."

"Don't worry," said Cleve. "We've got backup. If Bill Dick finds that blow on his desk, he'll be up here looking for me in a Jew York minute."

"Ah, the ugly head of anti-Semitism erects itself again."

"That ain't the ugly head I'm worried about. I just want to be damn sure that guy's left the club."

We wandered through the shadowy dressing room until Cleve hit the lights. No sign of any culprit lurking anywhere. Just empty beer bottles, leftover food, detritus from the previous evening's band.

"Jesus Christ," I said, "don't you have a daytime janitor?"

"You're looking at him," said Cleve.

As Cleve pulled open the big metal grating that led out to the balcony and the iguana, I thought I heard a slight stirring from the dumper area behind us. As reassuring daylight flooded into the dank dressing room, I shrugged it off and walked with Cleve onto the roof area overlooking Fifth Avenue.

"Yep," said Cleve, "that big ol' lizard's still up here."

"Better than my big ol' lizard being up here."

"Don't be too sure. You should see the broads flock around this monster. There's something about him that really turns them on. Maybe it's all those sexy green scales. I think he's got more groupies than you do."

"I'm not jealous," I said. "If I can reach one person out there I think I'm a success."

At that precise moment, a loud report came from somewhere inside the club. Almost at the same time the monster let out with a high-pitched, unearthly wail, which, it soon dawned upon us, was the sound of a bullet ricocheting off the metal scales of the creature.

"I think you just reached one person," said Cleve, ducking behind the iguana's hind legs.

"Long as he doesn't reach us," I said as I hit the deck. "There's no way off of this roof without a parachute. What the hell do we do now?"

"Follow me," said Cleve.

"I followed your ass up here," I said, nervously looking over the top of the iguana's giant right rear claw.

"Well, stand by your man."

"Or, in this instance, lie beside my man."

"We'll go to the only place we can safely hide."

"Where's that?"

"Inside the creature," said Cleve, slithering on his stomach slightly closer to Fifth Avenue.

When we were directly under the iguana's belly, Cleve reached up and unfastened a latch and a hatchlike door opened, sort of like the entrance to an upside-down submarine. With the latch for cover, we both levered and scrambled ourselves inside the metal monster. We were both red-lining in the adrenaline department when we closed the latch and sat down in there like two junked-out Jonases inside the whale.

"Stay low," said Cleve. "This big bastard's ugly but he ain't necessarily bulletproof."

"I'll keep that in mind," I said as I flattened myself out somewhere along the creature's lower intestine.

No sooner had I done that than three more shots came at us in rapid succession. We hugged the stomach lining of the iguana and waited several lifetimes, but all we heard was the sound of horns and traffic along Fifth Avenue. The insides of the monster were beginning to take on the ambience of an Indian sweat lodge, but where we were seemed a lot safer than where we weren't. We waited a little longer and then at last we heard voices. Prominent among them was Bill Dick bitching about all the commotion disturbing his customers.

"Two weeks ago you got shot at in a taxi," said Cleve, as he shakily lowered the hatch. "Then somebody blows up your loft. Now we've just had the attack on Fort Iguana. How in the hell do you get yourself into these kinds of situations?"

"Just lucky, I guess," I said.

Indeed, I felt as lucky as Charles Lindbergh when I stepped out of the iguana onto the terra firma of the Lone Star roof. Strangely enough, I remembered the time in Austin when Sammy Allred, Dylan Ferrero, and I, all of us so high we'd have needed three stepladders to scratch our asses, had seen a flick on Lindbergh's famous flight. In the movie, as Lindbergh is approaching Paris after flying thirty-six hours, he removes his goggles, opens a brown paper bag, and eats his lunch. It was at this point in the flick that Dylan had commented: "Look at the guy. He's half an hour from the finest restaurants in the world and he pulls out a ham sandwich."

35

The couch circuit can be a difficult one for any poor cowboy to work, especially in New York City in the wintertime. And I not only had to sleep around a lot, but I'd also felt it might be best foot forward to alter my habits and lifestyle as much as possible. In other words, I was seeking a lifestyle that did not require my presence. In my mind I could imagine how unpleasant the headlines might be if I got blown away at Big Wong's or the Monkey's Paw like a poor man's Mafia don. So I attempted to frequent new places and to crash for only a few nights at a time in one locus. Quite by accident I'd become what you might call the perfect housepest. I'd invariably bug out for the dugout after only a few days. Housepests that stay for more than three days always wind up smelling like a thousand-year-old Chinese fish egg.

I started out, reasonably enough, bunking with the Bakerman, but while the ambience was considerably improved over Ratso's digs, the place was about as big as your nose, not to mention the fact that Baker would often bring in a cute little booger and I'd have to choose between becoming a professional voyeur or taking a long, chilly walk in the middle of the night. I tried a little of both and found neither to be a very satisfying experience.

After several Bakerman hose-a-thons and several midnight walks, I moved on up to Chinga's new place on Central Park South. It was spacious accommodations compared to Baker's place, but the overriding problem with Chinga's place was that it had Chinga in it. Also, as my friend Dr. Jim Bone used to say, there were "a lot of rules for such a small company." Chinga smoked pot like a row of Mary Poppins chimneys, but he'd become highly agitato if I tried to puff a cigar in his apartment. His grooming mechanism appeared to be going awry again, and there seemed to be a penchant on his part for the almost incessant locking of pinkies. On top of all this, there was a rather high degree of paranoia about Chinga that manifested itself in forbidding any visitors, turning away routine deliveries, and screening all phone calls. The paranoia part didn't bother me. When you're a housepest and your life is clearly in danger, a guy like Chinga can make for a pretty gracious host, always provided that his behavior doesn't cause you to take a Brodie.

Both at Tom Baker's and at Chinga's, I'd tried repeatedly to reach Rambam and Judy. I'd left messages for both, but they'd seemed to have blipped off the screen. By day three at Chinga's I had a choice of either getting out or hanging myself from the rather ornate shower rod. I noticed, as well, to my personal horror, that I myself was beginning to exhibit unmistakable symptoms of a grooming mechanism gone awry.

It was at a midtown bar called Costello's, a bar frequented by journalists, that I spotted a familiar-looking member of the Fourth Estate. I was having a Jameson Irish Whiskey and he was having a Vodka McGovern.

"Hey, Kink," said McGovern. "Where you living these days?"

"In this bar," I said.

"That's funny," said McGovern. "So am I."

Though McGovern did spend quite a good bit of time in Costello's, it eventually emerged, after a countless number of additional rounds, that he had a place of his own, to which I proceeded to retire along with him. McGovern's place was in the Village on Jane Street, just across from a garden that proudly sported the last working windmill in New York City. His apartment was not quite up to Ratso's in terms of degeneracy or disarray, but certainly was not without a charm and eccentricity all its own. We weren't there long before McGovern got down to business.

"Okay," he said. "This is off the record now."

"What the hell are you yapping about?"

"This mysterious psycho who's trying to kill you. The guy you were telling me about in Costello's. The one who blew up your loft that night when you thought he was after Abbie Hoffman. That's the story. Is he after Abbie? Is he after you? How do you catch him before he catches you? It'd make a great story and I'm the guy who could write it. I might even be able to help you."

"Off the record," I said, "how?"

"Never underestimate the power of the press. There's all kinds of ways to fuck with this guy's mind—"

"Not to mention *my* mind—"

"—and to draw him out of the woodwork. Do you know who he is, for instance? Do you know his motive?"

"Off the record," I said, "no and no."

"And there may be other ways we can help you."

"What do you mean 'we'? You got a mouse in your pocket?"

"I mean your friends. I've been doing a little legwork already, you see. That prepubescent PI Rambam you've been plotting with. The ever-loyal Ratso. Tom Baker, troublemaker. Your friend Chinga who likes to lock pinkies."

"How'd you know about that?"

"Can't reveal our sources. And you've got another friend you might've overlooked."

"Judas Iscariot?"

"Not quite," said McGovern, laughing his too-loud-for-indoors Irish laugh. "The other friend you have is me. You seem to be in a hell of a jam. The story sounds too outlandish for the cops and they're never much help until after the fact. And after the fact might be too late. How about accepting a little help from your friends? We could form a kind of informal paramilitary group. We could call ourselves Kinky's Commandos."

"Weak name," I said.

"Don't worry," said McGovern. "We may not be all that much help."

In spite of myself, I was strangely touched by the offer from the big Irishman. I *was* in a hell of a jam. The guy in the army jacket who called himself John knew more about me than I knew about him. What could it hurt to recruit a little help? Besides, there was something about McGovern that made you know you could trust him. So before the night was over, I'd told him everything I knew and some of what I suspected.

"Is this on the record," he asked, "or off the record?"

"It can be on the record," I said. "But check with me before you print anything."

"It's a wise decision," said McGovern. "It's exactly where Jesus fucked up."

"What're you talking about?"

"He was a great teacher," said McGovern, "but He just didn't publish."

36

The following day I arose like Lazarus from McGovern's large pink davenport, an article of furniture that, he claimed, had traveled twice across the Atlantic. I was just in time to witness the morning sun spilling across the fire escape into Carole Lombard's eyes. Carole didn't mind, of course. As one of McGovern's patron saints, apparently, her picture hung on the wall all by itself next to his little fireplace. There was a small fire burning in the fireplace and a somewhat larger one in Lombard's eyes, but neither seemed to really warm the apartment a hell of a lot. McGovern, however, seemed not to notice. Working in shirtsleeves, he made some excellent coffee and added a small sidecar of Bushmill's to the project.

"So you feel pretty sure now," said McGovern, "that this guy's not after Abbie. You think he's after you."

"I can see him mistaking me for Abbie in the taxicab after he saw Abbie wearing a black cowboy hat. What I can't see is him mistaking Abbie for a large green iguana. After the shooting incident at the Lone Star, I think we have to conclude Abbie's out of it."

"I tend to agree with you, but what about your girlfriend Judy? I've met her a few times at the Paw, but just how much credence do you give to her supposed sightings of her dead flyboy lover?"

"About as much credence as I give to your sightings of Carole Lombard. She's now under the treatment of a shrink named Richard Bock. I'm not sure if he's really a shrink. He may just be a psychologist who wants to be a shrink when he grows up."

"Every schoolboy's dream," laughed McGovern.

"By the way, Judy's shrink is also Abbie's shrink. Quite cosmic, I thought."

"He'll also probably be *your* shrink if we don't find this John character pretty fast. Why don't we call a meeting of Kinky's Commandos?"

"Because I hate that name," I said.

It was later that morning, after knocking over a Chrysler Building-sized pile of old newspapers, that I picked up the blower and received a much welcome call from Rambam. Several days ago I'd left a brief account of the Lone Star action on his answering machine and he claimed he'd been in investigative high gear ever since. For one thing, he said, it'd taken a great deal of detective work merely to find me. He'd called Ratso, who'd referred him to Baker, who'd referred him to Chinga, who'd referred him to McGovern. At least, he said, he'd avoided locking pinkies with Chinga.

I filled Rambam in a little more regarding the episode with Cleve and the iguana and I told him about the supposed old war buddy of mine named John, who'd been asking Tommy the bartender about me at the Monkey's Paw. There was a lengthy silence on the line. Rambam was either thinking things over or freeing the hostages.

"Look," he said finally, "this psycho's directed violence toward you four times already. The thing with the big lizard, the grenade in your loft, the shot at the taxicab—that wasn't a bad shot, by the way—"

"I'll tell the guy next time I see him—"

"—and I'm also convinced those shots at Abbie in the cowboy hat were meant for you. As was the anti-Semitic threatening phone call."

"That I can live with."

"I hope you're right. Either this guy's Mr. Magoo or you've been very fucking lucky. We can't take a chance on him getting you in his crosshairs again. I think we need a preemptive strike of some kind."

"That's what the Bakerman suggested."

"Well, for once he's right."

I lit a cigar and watched the large form of McGovern lumber into his tiny dumper, apparently for some additional morning ablutions. Calling a preemptive strike on one psycho in a city where there's twelve million of them walking around was not going to be the quickest thing on the menu. Half the burned-out hippies in the world lived in New York and all of them had long hair and wore old army jackets. All of them were probably named John, too, I reflected as I waited for the Oracle of Brooklyn to speak again.

"And I was doing a little fact-check on your girlfriend Judy."

"Judy?"

"You remember her," said Rambam. "When she's not busy hosing your buddies she's busy either seeing her dead boyfriend or seeing her shrink."

"Psychologist."

"Proctologist," said Rambam. "Whatever. This Tim, however, is almost certainly dead. Courthouse records in North Carolina say he's buried there and I expect to hear at any time from the graves registration people in Honolulu. They're the ones who can give us an official identification of the body. But that's not what's bothering me."

"That's not what's bothering me, either. It's the grunting noises McGovern's making."

"Then try this one on for size. Let's just assume for the sake of argument that the moon is made of gefilte fish and Judy's old boyfriend Tim is still alive. Do you realize that, according to the same local courthouse records, Judy wasn't just Tim's girlfriend?"

"Don't tell me she was his sister. That was Ratso's theory."

"Well, Virginia, your little friend Ratso was wrong. She wasn't Tim's sister. She was Tim's wife."

"Jesus."

"No, Moses," said Rambam. "Now ask yourself the following question: 'Is she really worth breaking a commandment over?'"

"There's only one commandment I may have broken and it's not one of God's. It's my friend Sammy Allred's first commandment."

"Which is?"

"Never put your pencil and your dick on the same desk."

37

Since McGovern was one of the few adult Americans living in New York City who did not possess an answering machine, any attempts on Judy's part to reach me might well have been missed. When you're crashing with McGovern you tend not to go to a lot of picnics, museums, Broadway openings, or bridal showers, but that didn't necessarily mean the two of us stayed exclusively in the apartment like Emily Dickinson and her dog, Austin. There were frequent forays to Chinatown, not to mention an almost yo-yo-like grid of activity that ran from McGovern's place to the nearby Corner Bistro and back again in the straightest line between two pints. By the time Judy did reach me it was late on the following afternoon, and I'd had a lot of time to think things over. This avalanche of cerebration did not, however, make me a particularly smarter or wiser bear.

McGovern and I were drinking Vodka McGoverns in tall glasses as the phone began ringing and in the confusion of both of us trying to simultaneously tackle the blower, McGovern managed to step on that unfortunate instrument. When at last I picked it up, Judy sounded moderately irritated but none the worse for wear.

"What in the hell took you so long?" she shouted.

"A large mammal stepped on the telephone."

"I've been trying to reach you for days. I called Ratso and he referred me to Tom Baker—"

"You stopped in for a haircut—"

"Don't get cute. He referred me to Chinga. Chinga referred me to McGovern. And then the phone just rang and rang and rang."

"Like wedding bells," I said.

"I've been up here in Westchester for the week," Judy went on obliviously, "as part of a seminar and hot-tub therapy program that Dr. Bock recommended. It's called 'Letting Go of the Past.'"

"Have you?"

"God, I hope so. I think so, Kinky."

"Maybe I'll have to make it up to Westchester one of these days."

"It won't be in time. The professor who's running the seminar is going back to L.A. tomorrow."

"They always do," I said. "Of course, I doubt if the program would've done me much good anyway. It's hard to let go of the past if you can't even remember it."

"Do you think you can remember to meet me for dinner tonight? I'm coming into the city this evening and I'll just stop by my place to drop off some things, and then I could meet you at McGovern's."

"Smells good from here," I said.

I gave her McGovern's address and apartment number and hung up the blower just as McGovern put a new head on my Vodka McGovern. Like any good reporter working his home turf, he was naturally curious about the phone call.

"What's this about letting go of the past?" he wanted to know.

"Some hot-tub seminar Judy's taking in Westchester."

"Why are hot-tub seminars always in someplace like Westchester?"

"Because if you gave a hot-tub seminar in New Jersey nobody would come."

"Do you think it's really important whether or not you let go of the past?"

"Since I'm a person of the Jewish persuasion, let me give you the tedious, evasive, Talmudic answer to your question. Do *you* think it's really important to let go of the past?"

"Hell no," laughed McGovern. "I'm hanging on for dear life."

"Of course you don't happen to be hunted and haunted by an imaginary dead boyfriend."

"I'll stick with pink elephants," said McGovern.

I hung around McGovern's place for the rest of the afternoon and that wasn't a lot of place to hang around. In a way I missed the wide-open spaces of the loft on Vandam Street. Unfortunately, it was largely missing a second-floor flat. Peculiar that I should now begin to think of it as a flat. Tom Baker always called it a flat. I called it a loft. Baker called it a flat because that's what they called it in England and he wanted to be thought of as a more cosmopolitan person than

I was, which, of course, he was. Anybody was a more cosmopolitan person than I was. But when you're close to somebody a little of it always rubs off. If you've ever spent any time loitering around in a veterinarian's waiting room you'll notice that the humans and their animal companions all seem to bear distinct similarities to each other. You'll never see, for instance, a big, fat, easygoing woman, or man, as the case may be, come in with a skinny, ferret-faced, highly agitato dog, or cat, as the case may be. If you see a sad man, he'll have a sad dog. Even their eyes'll look the same. If a neurotic, unpleasant woman comes in, she'll be with a neurotic, unpleasant cat. Or dog, as the case may be. An old man will have an old dog. A frisbee-throwing nerd will have a golden retriever with a blue or red bandanna around its neck, depending upon the gender of said retriever. Or you might see an elderly couple, openly sobbing carrying in a burlap bag between them the body of a seventeen-year-old German shepherd that has just been put to sleep, as we say. The body is large and the bag is heavy and a young assistant comes up and offers to help, but they take it all the way themselves to their Olds 88. They want to carry it themselves. I suppose they always will. The world is a lot like a veterinarian's waiting room. Lots of people. Lots of animals. Lots of life and death and sickness. Lots of waiting. Bills to pay. Balls to cut. Raining cats and dogs. Noah's ark again.

"Maybe I ought to get a dog," I said to McGovern. "I'm getting tired of people."

"In New York?" said McGovern. "A dog's ridiculous. You need something that doesn't mind staying alone all day in an apartment, which, of course, you also don't have at the present."

"But I'll have to live someplace eventually."

"A dog is still a bad idea in the city."

"Okay, I'll get a cockroach."

"Now you're talking," said McGovern. "You could name him Franz."

"*I'm* starting to feel like Kafka myself. I know that guy's out there waiting for me. I know something's going to happen."

"You *have* talked to the cops?"

"I talked to them after the thing at the loft and again after the attack on Fort Iguana. They thought that one was pretty funny and I guess it did have its moments. But they felt there was too little to go on. The cop said he'd check it out if I checked out."

"Bad cop," said McGovern. "No donut."

38

I jumped into McGovern's microscopic rain room and took a shower. In anticipation of my dinner date with Judy, I sang a somewhat attenuated medley of the three greatest songs ever written. First, of course, was "Danny Boy." The Brits could take over and run every government on the face of the earth but they couldn't write "Danny Boy." The second song was "Waltzing Matilda," written by Australian Banjo Patterson in 1896 and still able to evoke the wild spirit of that faraway, redolent-of-dreams, on-the-beach land nearly everyone wishes to go to, and, when they're old, regrets they never made it. The third song I sang, and quite possibly the saddest, was "My Old Kentucky Home," written, of course, by a guy who died in a gutter in New York.

When I got out of the rain room and dried myself off with a half-damp towel lying on the radiator, I brushed my choppers and brushed my moss with what I thought was McGovern's hairbrush but later learned was some kind of toilet-bowl-cleaning implement. It didn't make much difference anyway. You can hide a worldful of things under a cowboy hat.

I was living out of my busted valise these days and also it was cold as hell in McGovern's apartment, so I got dressed pretty quickly and then joined my host for another Vodka McGovern. Then McGovern went out for a while. Then he came back again. Then he went out again and I was beginning to realize that apparently Judy was going to be late for our date. Eventually, McGovern came back again, but still no Judy.

"How long does it take," I asked him, "to get from Westchester to Manhattan?"

"It'd take me about two minutes," he said, "but some people never make it at all."

"What the hell could've happened to Judy?"

"I don't know," said McGovern, "but if she's not here by now I'm betting she doesn't win, place, or show."

"But she seemed really psyched about getting together tonight."

"Don't feel so bad," said McGovern. "It isn't every guy who can say he was stood up for a dead boyfriend."

"I've got a funny feeling this stiff might turn out to be a pretty lively corpse."

It was creeping rather close to Cinderella time when I decided to call Judy's apartment, but the phone just rang and rang and rang. It didn't sound like wedding bells, however. It sounded like the funeral of a friend in the rain.

I was debating whether to go to the Corner Bistro with McGovern or stay and beat myself to death with the toilet-bowl implement when two things happened at once. The phone rang and the front door buzzer sounded. It was an overload of activity for McGovern's apartment, but somehow we were able to handle it.

"You grab the phone," said McGovern. "I'll get the door."

"In another life," I said, "you might've made a fine executive."

"Another good reason," said McGovern as he walked to the door, "for not believing in reincarnation."

I excavated the blower from under a pile of old *New York Times*es and *Washington Post*s just in time to hear the stentorian tones of a familiar-sounding voice. It was Rambam.

"Big news," he said. "I just heard from Honolulu."

"Don Ho wants me on his show?"

"Very funny," said Rambam, "but not as funny as this. My contact on the Joint Military Graves Registration Unit now has confirmation of a positive ID on the body. Lt. Tim Petzel was definitely Judy's husband, was definitely shot down over three years ago in Vietnam, was definitely missing in action for several years, and was definitely located, identified, sent back, and buried last year in a military cemetery in North Carolina. That means he's definitely dead. It also means that if your girlfriend thinks she's seen him in New York this year, she definitely has a few too many pigeons on her antenna."

"I'll tell her when I see her."

"Be my guest."

"Right now I'm McGovern's guest, but I'm beginning to suspect that you might possibly make a more gracious host."

McGovern now was drunkenly ranting into the small call box beside the door. The sound emanating from that little box sounded like the mating call of a seal and its unintelligible nature appeared to further aggravate McGovern who now seemed to be mounting periodic attacks upon the entire wall.

"WHO THE FUCK IS IT?" he shouted.

"What the hell's going on?" asked Rambam.

"It appears to be a case of aggravated assault by a large Irishman upon a small sheet of perforated metal covering an apparently faulty intercom device connected to the front door of this building."

"GODDAMNIT!" roared McGovern, pounding on the wall. "IDENTIFY YOURSELF, YOU SORRY BASTARD!"

"Better go down and check it out," said Rambam. "Maybe it's Don Ho."

I thanked Rambam rather tersely, hung up the blower, and tried to navigate past McGovern into the narrow doorway. This operation was not as successful as it looked on the seed packet. By this time both McGovern and myself were running out of charm and I did not feel like performing square dance steps with a large, intoxicated Irishman in a tiny vestibule. As far as McGovern was concerned, I could pretty well see in his eyes that the ephemeral, carefree days of being his colorful Jewish housepest could almost be at an end.

Eventually, I got past McGovern, down the stairway, down the little hall, and out the front door. A pale, ghostly presence stood shivering on the stone steps of the building. As if to ward off the demons of the New York night, the wraithlike figure was wearing a red jacket with a little hood pulled up over its head.

"This isn't grandmother's house," I said.

39

As Judy painfully pulled back the little hood, even by the low light of the streetlamp I could see the blood on her face. As she took a step closer I could see that somebody had really messed her up pretty good. Violence is not an uncommon thing in the city or even in the countryside, but the face of urban crime often seems particularly unattractive. In New York, Little Red Riding Hood doesn't always make it through the woods.

"Judy," I said. "What happened?"

Her answer was to sway slightly so that I could see the ugly swelling on the left side of her face and then to pass out in my arms. I half-dragged her toward the door which had now closed and locked behind me. I searched frantically for the buzzer to McGovern's apartment. For security reasons the buttons were not in any numerical or alphabetical order. It was a wonder, I thought, that McGovern ever got into his own apartment.

It was apartment 2B or, as McGovern was fond of saying, "2B or not to be." That was indeed the question. I held the button down and shouted into the intercom.

"McGovern," I said. "Let me in!"

"So you say," said McGovern.

"Goddamnit, it's Kinky. Judy's with me. I tell you she's hurt!"

"Felch alert?" asked McGovern.

"McGovern, if you don't open this goddamn door—"

But at that moment the door buzzed open and Judy's eye fluttered several times. I say "eye" because her left eye was swollen shut and all I could see was her right. There was such a wild, bewildered look in it that I was almost glad I couldn't see the other one.

Though her consciousness had returned, it was still like escorting a walking zombie down the narrow corridor, with Judy not seeming to know or care where I was taking her. In the bright, garish lighting of the hallway I could see a ghastly laceration on the left side of her head with blood the color of a red neon exit sign. Given her current demeanor and the grievous extent of her injuries, she could well be in a state of shock.

"Who did this to you, Judy?" I said, as I half-guided, half-carried her up the little stairway.

"Who do you think?" she said, in a flat, almost frightening monotone.

"My guess would be Larry Holmes," I said, watching her carefully for reaction.

"My guess would be Larry Holmes," she repeated in a soft, disquieting voice that sounded dangerously close to that of a dying child.

Once I'd gotten her into the apartment, McGovern had another surprise in store for me. He magically metamorphosed from a raging, unpredictable devil to the Florence Nightingale of the West Village. Before I could wring my hands properly McGovern had placed her on the couch, treated her for possible shock by elevating her feet and covering her with a blanket, and examined and dabbed at her wounds with a warm washcloth. He spoke to her gently and she seemed to be conversing with him and behaving more normally. As McGovern prepared her a special "Old World recipe" hot toddy, I found a tall glass and prepared myself another Vodka McGovern.

"Do you think we should get her to a hospital?" I said.

"She'll be fine once she gets this down her," said McGovern, throwing ingredients into the hot toddy like a mad alchemist.

"You don't look like a skinny Jewish doctor or a fat black nurse," I said. "You sure you know what you're doing?"

"Are you kidding? Just get out of my way."

"Yes, Dr. Numbnuts. But what if she's exhibiting symptoms of shock?"

"Get out of my way or I'll exhibit myself to the patient. That'll really put her in shock. In the meantime, Inspector Maigret, why don't you get busy and find out who did this to her?"

"I'll hop right on it."

I took myself and the Vodka McGovern to an overstuffed easy chair, sat down sulkily, and watched McGovern minister to the patient. I had to admit he looked like he knew what he was doing. In a matter of moments McGovern was motioning me over to the davenport.

"It wasn't Larry Holmes," said Judy. "It was Tim."

McGovern looked at me. I rolled my eyes upward toward Carole Lombard and she either winked at me or else it was a very strong Vodka McGovern.

"Tim is dead, Judy," I said. "We now have official confirmation of that."

"That's just what he said before he hit me with the gun. I think he would've shot me right in the hallway of my apartment but he heard people running up so he just hit me a few times with the gun."

"Thoughtful fellow," said McGovern.

"What exactly did he say to you?" I asked.

"He said: 'Tim is dead. You just don't believe it yet. But ya'll will.'"

"Ya'll?" said McGovern to me in something of a loud stage whisper.

"That's the southern pluperfect plural," I said.

"It sounds dangerously like it includes you, kemosabe."

"Judy," I said, "what did Tim look like?"

"Just the same as he did before the war," she answered almost wistfully.

"You gotta help me with this, Judy," I said. "I wasn't in the war. I was in the Peace Corps. What exactly did he look like tonight? Describe Tim to me."

Even before Judy spoke a word I realized that, in the tradition of all great detectives, I'd been an idiot. Like Sherlock Holmes, who, incidentally, was no relation to Larry Holmes, I'd been a total fool, an imbecile. Like Hercule Poirot, I'd been the ox, the jackass, the very embodiment of virtually every large, slow-moving barnyard animal, none of which, however, seem quite as dense or dull-witted as a fictional detective who's missed an obvious clue by making an all-too-human mistake. Like Sherlock and Poirot, I was in many ways a fictional detective. Half the game, it seemed, was in my mind; the other half was as real as Judy's blotched and bruised and battered face staring wanly up at me from that hideous lox-colored davenport, which had sailed twice across the ol' herring pond, back and forth from a fabled land with a timeless moor where Holmes would forever be an elderly, eccentric keeper of bees and a timeless mirror where Poirot would forever be an anal, anonymous little man waxing a meticulously kept mustache that time had turned as silver as the mirror of our lives. There is a razor-thin line between fiction and nonfiction and often, indeed, it must be erased to get at the truth of human nature.

I'd made a classic mistake. I'd assumed that a clean-cut Navy flyer would fit that relative, generic description before, during, and after the war. I'd taken him as a military type. I hadn't been listening when Judy'd first told me about supposedly encountering him outside The Ear. "He looked just like he did before the war," she'd said. Wars change men. Wars change women. Wars change everything. I'd made a classic mistake, all right. It had almost resulted in events of near-Greek tragic proportions.

"Come on, Judy," I coaxed her. "What did Tim look like when he attacked you tonight?"

"Like he did before the war," she said. "A little thinner, I thought. His face was gaunt, scary-looking."

"What about his hair?" I said, with a slight confirmatory nod to McGovern.

"Long blond hair," she said.

"Eyes?"

"Blue as the sky," said Judy.

40

"Whatta ya mean 'Tim's alive'?" shouted Rambam, when I got him over the blower the next morning.

"Just what I said," I said, as I sipped on an excellent cup of McGovern-made coffee and puffed on a cigar. "Tim's alive."

Judy was still crashed out on the long pink davenport, and that was fine with me. I didn't want her going out without an armed infantry battalion after what I now suspected. Indeed, the streets very probably weren't going to be much safer for me either, the way things looked. Crime was really up in the city.

"The Graves Registration Unit doesn't make many mistakes, Kinky," said Rambam. "Their labs are very thorough, and when they make a positive ID you can be pretty damn sure it's a positive ID. Maybe your girlfriend's imagining things again. Maybe, in reality her assailant was a large black man in a ski mask."

"That doesn't quite fit her description of the guy," I said.

"In fact, her description of Tim perfectly fits the guy who's been after *my* ass, the same one you saw running from the loft after the grenade attack on Fort Friedman. It's the same guy, Rambam. And, believe me, he *is* alive."

"I don't know if he's the same guy or not," said Rambam. "All I know is Tim's probably dead."

I glanced around the small apartment. McGovern had gone out for groceries, and without his large presence blocking the sun, the place looked just a tad roomier. It was still a small apartment, though. A small apartment in a small world where small twists of fate made all the great differences between men and nations. I was going to have a hell of a time convincing Rambam or anybody else of the scenario I suspected had occurred. I wasn't even completely sure myself. I thought I very possibly knew *why*. I just couldn't figure out *how*.

Social intercourse wound down with Rambam reminding me to keep Judy and myself indoors or very low profile for a few days until he came up with a plan of action. I didn't really feel in a mood to be taking Anne Frank lessons and I told Rambam so.

"Why the hell do we have to stay in McGovern's cramped, claustrophobic quarters," I wanted to know, "if the guy is *probably* dead?"

"Because the guy is *probably* dead," said Rambam.

I cradled the blower and, with Judy still sleeping and McGovern still out shopping, used the moment to reflect quietly upon the situation. I stared across McGovern's little fire escape into the alley below and the city beyond. Somewhere out there, I knew in my heart, Tim or John or some wretched warhorse without a name was stubbornly grazing nearby, waiting patiently to trample my dreams. My only hope was to wake up from this nightmare in time to decipher his true identity. There was no doubt that the military experts had compelling reasons to believe Tim was worm-bait in some bone orchard in North Carolina. But military intelligence, as any Jewish cowboy could tell you, has always been a contradiction in terms. All I had to do was figure out how they'd made such a potentially fatal mistake.

It was obvious, at least to me, that Tim and John were the same person. I also believed that person was the same person Judy had once been briefly married to. Unless, of course, she was totally cookin' on another planet. These minor details could wait for explanation, however, until some of last night's trauma had worn off. The larger question still loomed ominously over the skyline of our little lives: How could Lt.Tim Petzel crawl out of the grave bent upon placing Judy and myself into said grave? I felt I had the answer to the part about croaking me and Judy. How he'd crawled out of the grave was something I'd have to look up when I got home. If I'd had a home.

Just as I was on the cusp of a strange new idea, Nurse McGovern burst in the door laden with groceries, products to speed the patient's convalescence, and a large bottle of Jameson Irish Whiskey to speed my convalescence. There was a certain poignancy about this large man full of determination to be nothing more than a friend and a thoughtful host. If there were more McGoverns in this world, I thought, there would be less reason for all the Tims.

If I did somehow see this current unpleasantness to a successful conclusion it would be a minor miracle, I figured, but at least I'd have solved my first case as an amateur private investigator. Then I could give up my night job at the Lone Star which was barely covering the Peruvian-marching-powder bills. It seemed to me that if I could but answer two questions, I might have a chance at catching Tim before he croaked me and prevented me from ever becoming an amateur private investigator in the first place. The questions were: Out of twelve million people in New York, why was Tim gunning for me and Judy? And, since it was obvious that this was his mission, how did he and his gun get out of the bone orchard where he belonged? I thought I had the answer to the first question. It was conjecture, but it was based on Jewish radar and cowboy logic and it sounded close enough for country dancin'. As far as the second question was concerned, God only knew the answer.

Since God had created one of those flukishly rare, mild, beautiful, sunny winter days in New York, I figured I might just take a walk outside the walls of my little sanctuary and ask Him. I checked on Judy, who was still slumbering peacefully, and then I put on my hat and told McGovern my plans to take a little meditational stroll around the grounds. This notion did not please him.

"How do you know Tim's not waiting outside?" asked McGovern, not unreasonably. "How do you know he didn't follow Judy here last night?"

"Because the guy may be crazy but he cares enough for his own well-being not to want witnesses. That's what saved Judy from a bullet last night. He never would've followed her all the way over here. If I understand his motive and his mental state correctly, he would've definitely croaked her on the way. Therefore he didn't follow her over here last night."

"Good deductive reasoning, Sherlock," said McGovern. "I hope to hell you're right. How about a little farewell shot of Jameson's before your walk with God?"

McGovern poured out two hefty shots and handed me one. He clinked his glass against mine.

"How about an Irish toast?" said McGovern.

"Goes with the snake-piss," I said.

"May the best of the past be the worst of the future," he said.

"That's beautiful, McGovern," I said. "But I wish that just for once the past would do us all a big favor and stay right where it is."

41

I hadn't walked more than a block when it started to rain. It was a strange kind of a rain, because the sun just kept right on shining as if it weren't happening. The sun and the rain both acted like they didn't give a damn and I didn't give a damn either, so that made three of us. You could see raindrops sliding down the windows with the sun shining through them. You could see a guy in a black cowboy hat walking down a street who didn't care if a raindrop-shaped bullet shined right through him.

"The devil is beating his wife," I said to myself, which is what you're supposed to say to yourself when it's raining and the sun is shining, always provided, of course, that you're still on speaking terms with yourself.

The devil in the piece, beyond a doubt, was Navy Lt. Tim Petzel. The battered wife without question was Judy. So the devil was beating his wife right now as the sun was shining while it was raining and the devil had beaten his wife last night as well, and most probably in this best of all possible worlds the devil would always be beating his wife, and who in their right mind wanted to get in the middle of a domestic squabble? If there's two things I can't stand, as Patrick O'Malley used to say, it's a shitty baby and a crying man. To that you could always add a good Samaritan. Unfortunately, by virtue of being Judy's supposed boyfriend, I was already in Tim's crosshairs, regardless of my good intentions or lack thereof. I didn't really care if I was perceived as a good Samaritan. What I hoped to avoid was being a dead Samaritan.

The past few months, I reflected, as I trudged up Hudson, had been quite a ball-dragger of an experience for me. There's nothing like having a dead guy come back and try to croak you. It almost makes you appreciate being alive. Such were my dark thoughts as I followed my footsteps unconsciously through the darker still canyons of New York real estate and ended up to my mild surprise in front of my old burned-out loft. It's better to have a burned-out loft than a burned-out mind, I figured, as my gaze wandered over the garbage trucks on parade and settled sadly on the blackened exterior of 199B Vandam Street. Nobody'd be living there for a while, probably. Too bad I hadn't burned up the place for insurance money. Now that I thought about it, a little Jewish lightning might not have been such a bad idea.

I was starting to walk away when I stepped on a twisted toy trumpet some kid had left out in the rain and almost broke my goddamn leg. I was lying in the gutter like Oscar Wilde, staring at the stars that no one else could see, when a dark, thin, unfriendly-looking woman strode purposefully out of the building and began to tape a sign to the front door. The sign read: "Fourth floor apartment for rent. Call Zorka." A phone number had been provided.

"Hold the weddin'," I said, as I climbed out of the gutter. "I might be interested in that apartment."

"There's a two-hundred-dollar security deposit," said the woman, studying me carefully. She did not appear to be enjoying her field of study.

"Why such a high security deposit?" I asked. The entire building, inside and out, was little more than an old warehouse.

"We're being a little more careful with prospective tenants," she said. "Some idiot on the second floor practically got himself blown up last month. Be a while before that one's ready for occupancy. Crazy bastard could've blown up the whole building."

"If not the world," I said.

"Some people," said the woman, starting to go back inside.

"I know what you mean," I said. "Look, I might be interested in the apartment. How long do you think it'll still be for rent?"

"Until some other mad scientist comes along," she said. "You want to look at it?"

So I went into the freight elevator with this saturnine creature who introduced herself as Zorka. The machine had just achieved liftoff when she seemed to remember that the guy who almost blew the whole place up was also a cowboy. I quickly introduced myself as Neil Shelby, a male model on my way to shoot a cowboy commercial for Calvin Klein. I wasn't a real cowboy, I assured her. If I'd been a real cowboy, I figured, I probably would've christianed her down on the security deposit.

Maybe it was looking down on all those garbage trucks, but something about the place brought back a wave of nostalgia for a past that I hadn't even liked very much. I remembered what Abbie had told me once about nostalgia: "Nostalgia," he'd intoned, "is a symptom of illness in an individual or a society."

I was pretty sure Abbie was right. Nostalgia was something to be avoided at all costs. Nevertheless, I agreed to sublet the place from the Zorka woman. Of course, the large pastel painting of the ballet dancer would have to go, but then, so would all the rest of us sooner or later.

As I walked out of there, somewhat poorer financially, but with the key to the new loft in my pocket, I felt infinitely richer in the coin of the spirit. I told myself it had nothing to do with nostalgia for the recent past. Maybe I'd just wanted a place to call my own. Maybe, like Abbie himself, I was getting tired of running. But when you've been running for a while, what you're really running from is never quite what you think it is. And what you're running to is never quite what you hope it is. Life itself, you inevitably find, is very much like the cardboard scenery in a spaghetti western; everybody drives around in Yom Kippur Clippers and they still won't give Jim Thorpe his fucking medals back. No one's ever won the human race but guys like Abbie sometimes make it fun to watch. Every hamster doesn't ride the wheel.

With these thoughts in mind, I walked along in the general direction of McGovern's place. But before I got there, something happened. I met a girl in a peach-colored dress.

42

She was standing outside a little bakery on Jane Street, holding two tiny dogs on leashes. She had a spectacularly beautiful American face upon the planes of which intelligence and innocence fought a pitched battle that looked like it might last a lifetime. She had rich-girl hair—long, straight, blond, thick—like she'd eaten only the best foods all her life. She had a peach-colored bow in her hair to match her outfit. Each of the little dogs had a bow as well. As the light rain glinted through the sunlight, the girl in the peach-colored dress gave the effect of a vision—impossibly fragile, ephemeral, childlike, so beautiful you could see right through her to a better world. It was not surprising, I reflected, that she appeared to be so childlike. She had to be all of six years old.

"Are you a *real* cowboy?" she asked, pausing perfectly to adjust the bow in her perfect hair. "Or are you just dressed up like one?"

Leave it to a kid to ask all the hard questions. Leave it to a kid to make you momentarily wonder if all your life you've been living a lie. Maybe she was seven.

"Of course I'm a real cowboy," I said, struggling for a measure of masculine indignancy. "Haven't you ever seen a real cowboy before?"

"Not in New York," she said.

The kid had a point there. She also had kind of a smart-ass edge to her that was starting to get up my sleeve. She was going to give some lucky bastard a hard time one of these days.

"We went to a dude ranch in Arizona when I was four," she continued. "They had some real cowboys there but they didn't look like you."

"You can't always tell a real cowboy just by looking at him," I said. It was too late to tell her I was a male model named Neil Shelby on my way to shoot a cowboy commercial for Calvin Klein. Besides, I wasn't.

"You mean real cowboys are like fairies?" she said, with that sudden earnest grasp of the truth that only childhood engenders.

"How old did you say you were?" I said, looking vaguely around for her mother.

"I didn't say," she said, "but I'll be six on August 14, and if you're wondering where my mother is, she's the well-dressed blond lady in that store who's watching you very carefully right now. Do real cowboys carry guns?"

"Of course not," I said. "We've always contended that if anybody wants to kill us, they have to bring their own gun. What's your name?"

"Stephanie," she said, kneeling down to introduce the dogs. "Holly. Dandelion. I want you to meet a real cowboy." The dogs, who were about half as high as my boots, seemed moderately interested. I hunkered down at a safe distance so as not to further agitate the well-dressed mother and I made a clumsy adult effort to relate to the nervous, rodent-sized creatures.

"They're cute little boogers," I said, "and so are you."

"Holly, you need Dandelion's pink ribbon," said Stephanie, as if I didn't exist. "It goes better with your collar, but the problem is I can't tie ribbons very well, so instead of changing your ribbon with Dandelion let's just give her your collar and Dandelion, you give Holly your collar. Then everything will be perfect."

With that, before my astonished eyes, her little fingers effortlessly removed Holly's collar, dog tag, leash, and all, and dexterously placed it upon Dandelion's slender neck. She then unfastened Dandelion's collar and, in less than the time it took me to light a cigar, she'd accomplished the entire little operation. It was quite an amazing thing to watch, actually. The kid knew at age six exactly what she was doing, which was a hell of a lot more than I could say for myself. There were, of course, many things the kid didn't know or understand yet. She probably couldn't tell you why we fought the war in Vietnam. I doubted very much if she knew that Turkish people once used to brush their teeth with urine. These are the kinds of things you pick up as you go along.

"For your information," said Stephanie, "Holly is now Dandelion and Dandelion is now Holly, but not really."

"I'll take that under review," I said, as Stephanie's mother came out of the bakery. "But they're so tiny I'd need my bird book and binoculars to tell them apart."

"Holly is a *Yorkie,*" said Stephanie, as if she were talking to the village idiot. "Dandelion is a *Maltese.* Malteses are always *white.* Yorkies are always *cute* with the *heart* of a *lion.*"

"Holly's a Yorkie," I repeated. "Dandelion's a—"

"Let's go, darling," said the well-dressed woman, giving me the wintriest of smiles.

The little girl and the two little dogs followed dutifully in her wake. It was a good thing that they did, because otherwise I might never have gotten to McGovern's house.

"Don't forget!" the little girl shouted over her shoulder. "Malteses are always white! Yorkies have the heart of a lion!"

"I'll remember that!" I shouted back, and indeed I would. It might come in handy some day if I was dog-sitting in hell.

As they rounded the corner on their way out of sight, Stephanie tossed her rich-girl hair in a very adult affectation, then gave me a friendly good-bye wave like the child that she was. When I see something like that I always wonder if the kid isn't growing up too fast. Of course, I've often wondered the same thing about myself.

As I ankled it up the sidewalk to McGovern's I was actually smiling, a rare enough occurrence in recent days. It was a beautiful afternoon. Besides, the final piece of a murderous mental mosaic had at last fallen into place. Red skies in the morning, sailor take warning.

By the time I'd gotten to McGovern's front steps I had the whole plan worked out. It was going to take a little cooperation and a little discretion and a little luck, but most of what I needed had already been given to me by a little girl. A little girl I probably would never see again.

Sometimes a very little thing can be a linchpin for everything else, a tiny, twinkling star around which swings a solar system. As I pushed the buzzer of 2B or not 2B, I thought of all the frenzied activity, all the human endeavor currently taking place in this building, this street, this city. I remembered something our old neighbor back in Texas, Earl Buckelew, had once said many years ago. A guy from the city had been looking over all the undeveloped acreage on Earl's ranch and at one point had asked him if the land was good for anything. "All it's good for," Earl had told him, "is to hold the world together."

43

"No!" shouted Judy. "Hell no, I'm not going to marry you!"

I hadn't been entirely sure she'd go for the plan but at least her spirited rejoinder indicated she obviously was feeling much better.

"I don't know how you could pass up an offer like this," I said, trying not to choke to death on my phlegm. "It must mean that you're still married to Tim."

Judy physically recoiled at these words just as McGovern came lumbering out of the bedroom. A major collision was narrowly averted. "I'm not still married to Tim," said Judy, stamping her little foot hard on the floor for emphasis.

"Please don't do that," said McGovern somewhat beseechingly. "The lady downstairs has been giving me a really hard time lately."

"Fuck the lady downstairs," said Judy with some intensity.

"I've been trying to for seven years," said McGovern coolly.

"How'd you know I'd been married to Tim?" asked Judy,

now leaning against the far wall under Carole Lombard's portrait. Both pairs of feminine eyes bore into me unmercifully.

"I wouldn't be much of a private investigator if I didn't know that," I said.

"You're not much of a private investigator," said Judy, "or you'd have caught Tim by now."

"I'll catch him," I said. "But first I'm going to ask you a few questions and I want a few truthful answers."

Judy, I sensed, would've liked to move farther away, but that, of course, was quite impossible. Her back was literally up against an exposed brick wall. I thought I knew pretty well where I was going with this, but I couldn't be entirely sure. If the truth be told, I was winging it. Just like Tim.

"For God's sake, Judy," I said, "be honest with me now. It might just save your life and mine."

"And I'd hate to lose two housepests," said McGovern.

Judy smiled at McGovern, then blinked back a tear or two, then, like Rapid Robert once said, she broke just like a little girl.

"Were you married to Tim before he left for Vietnam?" I asked her.

Judy nodded.

"Was the marriage having major problems, either between you and Tim or between either of you and your in-laws?"

Judy nodded again, this time a little sadly, I thought. It looked like I was coming in for a perfect night landing on the old aircraft carrier. But I had to be careful. The seas can play tricks on you.

"And Tim wanted a divorce, but you thought the two of you could work it out?"

Judy nodded again. McGovern stared on in amazement, possibly with a new respect for my investigative powers. But it wasn't investigative work that had brought this case so close to its solution. It was deductive reasoning. Deductive reasoning and the good fortune of meeting a girl in a peach-colored dress.

"He probably wrote you sporadically for a while, but after the plane went down you never heard from him or saw him again, not until you caught sight of him by accident in the alley behind the Ear. Is that correct?"

Apparently it was close enough for country dancing, because Judy put her hands to her face and the waterworks went into high gear.

"But what does it all mean?" she managed to sob.

"It means you and I have unintentionally gotten caught up in a very dangerous, near-fatal fraud. It means that we all have a lot of work to do and we'll have to do it fast. And finally, Judy, it means you'll have to marry me."

Judy looked at me like I was clinically ill. McGovern gazed straight ahead like somebody'd just hit him with a hammer. Even Carole Lombard seemed mildly surprised by my last statement. Judy, of course, had told the truth when she'd insisted she wasn't still married to Tim. She'd thought for some time that she was his widow. Because the marriage hadn't lasted long, because he'd gone to war and been shot down, and possibly because of his attitude toward the marriage as well, she'd glossed over the fact that she was Tim's widow, preferring to remember him as a long-lost boyfriend hero. Lots of things in life look better once they're relegated to the past tense.

But Judy, unfortunately, was not now nor had she ever been

a widow. Tim, unfortunately, was very much with us. And time, unfortunately, was not on our side. McGovern poured the three of us hefty shots of Château de Catpiss, then we sat down at his little table and I laid out my plan. If Tim had thought the war was over, he was very much mistaken.

"My word of honor as a furrier," I said. "We don't really have to get married. We just have to make everyone think we're going to. McGovern can be very helpful with this. I believe a highly publicized engagement party should be the perfect way, if I've ciphered his messed-up mind correctly, to trap this particular two-legged rat. He's tried to take out Judy and myself and so far he's failed. He's obviously desperate, for reasons I think I can guess. I can't see him drawing a bye on the chance to finally frag both of us together."

"This could turn into a shotgun wedding yet," said McGovern, and he poured us each another round. Then he lifted his glass in a toast.

"To the future," he said.

44

It was a little over a week later on a bright Sunday afternoon, and the Monkey's Paw was particularly well manicured for the big engagement party. Ratso and Chinga were the cohosts for the affair, McGovern had planted a big spread in the *Daily News,* and Rambam was in charge of security. Mick Brennan was the official photographer for the event and Pete Myers had planned to cater it from the kitchen in his own apartment. Cleve was providing what turned out to be a rather hideous country-rock band from New Jersey. It did not bode particularly well for the event that when I walked into the place every aforementioned individual was already so high they needed a large, rural family of stepladders to scratch their asses. The one exception was Rambam. That was because he wasn't there yet.

Tom Baker was the first actual guest to arrive, and he was definitely already out where the buses don't run when he got there. Because we'd rented the Paw for the special occasion, there was no problem bringing Baker or McGovern into the place. Getting them out would be another story, but, as McGovern always says, it wasn't my yob. My yob was to stand there and smile like a happy little fiancé as Mick Brennan took a rapid series of flash photos from a point about two inches away from my nose. By the time my intended arrived—some women do look good in black—practically everybody was walking on their knuckles from marching powder, whiskey, and gorilla biscuits. I was struggling to remain vertical myself. It isn't every day you attend your own engagement party.

Thankfully, most of the heavy groundwork had been done by now. I'd told Rambam how I suspected Tim had been able to come back from the dead. He checked it out, looked deeper into Tim's service record, and discovered that things were pretty much the way I'd thought they'd be. Of course he wasn't calling himself Tim anymore.

"What do you think of the decorations?" said Ratso. "Chinga and I worked very hard to enhance the ambience and give the affair just the right touch."

"It's bloody awful, mate," said Brennan. "Where'd you get these blue-and-white streamers and little Israeli flags?"

"From my nephew's bar mitzvah," said Ratso, admiring the setup. "Nobody'll notice."

"He's right about that," said Baker. "I especially like these cocktail napkins. 'Congratulations Randy and Kimberly.' What happened to Judy and Stinky? I mean Pinky. I mean Finky. I mean *Kinky?*"

"I didn't do the cocktail napkins," said Ratso. "That was Chinga's department."

"Well, the whole thing's bloody shithouse," said Ross Waby. "I've seen better-looking wakes."

"Which is what this occasion might become if anything goes wrong," said Rambam, as he took off his coat and pulled up a chair at the bar.

"Is the security in place?" I asked him furtively.

"It shouldn't be hard to spot the agents from the Office of Naval Intelligence," said Rambam. "They're the only clean-cut guys in the place. I stationed them at the door to catch him if he tries to crash the party. I notice half the street people in New York already have."

"We had to paper the house," said Chinga. "Kinky's not that popular."

"Where the hell's Judy?" I asked McGovern. "We've got to keep up some semblance of activity in the happy-couple department."

"That may prove a little difficult," said McGovern. "She just went into the men's room with Chinga and Tom Baker and what appeared to be enough marching powder to make a third-world nation mildly amphibious."

"Great," said Ratso. "Just when I have to take a Nixon."

"You could try the ladies'," said McGovern.

"That's worse, mate," said Mick Brennan. "An entire country-rock band from New Jersey's in there and it's bloody well not to just tune up their instruments."

"Where the hell's Cleve?" shouted Ratso. "We've gotta get some music going and I've got to take a Nixon."

"I really like your friends," said a rather bovine woman on her way out. "They've got a lot of class."

"Just like you've got a lot of ass, love," said Brennan.

"Come on," said a ferret-faced man next to her. "You're talking to my wife."

"I feel sorry for you, mate," said Brennan.

"You're sure this guy's showing up?" said Rambam from the next barstool.

"He's got to," I said. "It's either that or looking over my shoulder for the rest of my life."

"Well, don't look over your shoulder now," said Rambam. "I think Ratso's taking a dump in the cloakroom."

Two hours later, the place was full of celebratory people. Whether they knew, or suspected, or even gave a damn about the true nature of the function they were attending was anybody's guess. The country-rock band from New Jersey was up on the little stage playing "Orange Blossom Special" for about the fourteenth time. Tim was a no-show.

"I don't know why country-rock bands from New Jersey always have to play 'Orange Blossom Special,'" said Chinga.

"It's the way of their people," I said.

"Maybe they don't know 'Cum Stains on the Pillow (Where Your Sweet Head Used to Be),'" said McGovern.

"That must be it," said Baker. "They're culturally deprived. I've been trying to get 'em to play 'Proud to Be an Asshole from El Paso,' but the assholes don't even know *that* one."

"That's like not recognizing a Van Gogh," said Chinga. There was a certain stoic sadness in his voice. He was, after all, the author of the song.

"Where's your future ex-wife?" said Tom Baker.

"How the hell should I know," I said. "Maybe she's hanging from a shower rod in the men's room."

"Your attitude doesn't seem to bode well for a lifetime of marital bliss. Of course, who in their right mind wants a lifetime of marital bliss?"

"Right now I'd settle for the only guy in New York who really thinks this is an engagement party to walk in the door."

"This isn't really an engagement party?" said Baker. "I can't believe it. You've got to be shitting me. You two seemed like such a happy couple with a bright future to look forward to, Finky. I mean Pinky. I mean Stinky. I mean Kinky . . ."

But I wasn't really listening to the Bakerman at the moment. Even above the "Orange Blossom Special" I could hear shouting from the front of the Paw. A scuffle was clearly breaking out just at the foot of the front stairs. A late-arriving party guest was being forcibly subdued by two very efficient-looking, clean-cut guys at the doorway. They quickly put bracelets on the protesting guy. Then they removed a large, unpleasant-looking gun from under his old army coat.

"Throw him in the fuckin' brig!" shouted Rambam, as the Naval Intelligence officers hustled a somewhat dazed Tim Petzel out the door.

"Turn out the lights," said the Bakerman. "The party's over."

A slinky, sexy, green-eyed blonde slipped out of the crowd and began leaning a bit suggestively against the Bakerman's barstool.

"Or maybe," he said, winking for my benefit, "it's just getting started."

45

"Everyone's done his part in getting to the bottom of this insidious investigation," I said. "Rambam particularly has done some excellent background work."

"And Ratso particularly did a really superb job with the decorations for the engagement party," said Tom Baker.

"Get somebody else next time," said Ratso.

"There won't be a next time," I said.

It was later that same evening. The Navy had taken Tim Petzel away to be court-martialed for murder and I was explaining how it all came to pass for the benefit of the Bakerman and Ratso, who were sitting attentively on Ratso's skid-marked couch. It wasn't quite like addressing the multitudes, but you take what you can get.

"Tim Petzel," I continued, "is a murderer. He didn't succeed in killing Judy or me, not that he wouldn't've liked to. He also didn't die in a plane crash while on a mission, but he did frag several of his officers before he went AWOL in Vietnam.

This much Rambam has already dug up from contacts in Naval Intelligence."

"So he was Judy's husband at one time?" asked Ratso.

"Definitely. Though she gave him up for dead when she buried him. Most people do. Then, of course, no one was more surprised than Judy when she spotted him quite by accident alive in New York. Well, there was one person who was more surprised. That was Tim. He had to keep his new identity a secret, you see, so he vowed to do something about Judy and her nosy-parker boyfriend, yours truly. The Navy looks rather gravely, no pun intended, upon killing two officers and going AWOL from active duty during wartime."

"Wait a minute," said Baker. "Hold the funeral. If Tim was captured crashing the party today, who's buried in Grant's Tomb?"

"Luther Tibbs," I said.

The Bakerman looked at me. Ratso looked at me. The polar bear's head looked at me. The Virgin Mary looked at me. I struck a semi-Sherlockian pose, puffed patiently on a cigar, and gazed out the window into the middle distance of the all-too-mortal mind.

"Who the fuck is Luther Tibbs?" said Ratso at last.

"I thought you'd never ask," I said. "Luther Tibbs is a fellow flyboy of Tim Petzel's. Rather, he *was* a fellow flyboy of Tim Petzel's. Luther Tibbs is the one who went down in the plane, went missing for months, was officially ID'd as Tim Petzel, and currently resides in a military bone orchard in North Carolina."

"So Luther Tibbs became Tim Petzel," said Ratso excitedly, "and Tim Petzel became Luther Tibbs!"

"Excellent, Watson," I said. "You truly surpass yourself."

"Throw him a kipper," said Baker. "The fact is the military is right up there with the federal government, the FBI, and the CIA in terms of record-keeping, forensic labs, modern methods of identification of bodies. Not to mention the military has a bureaucratic net spreading all over hell's hundred acres. The long arm of military law might even exceed the boardinghouse reach of the feds."

"In other words," said Ratso, "how'd he do it?"

"Fate dealt him a lucky hand," I said. "He was unhappy in his marriage and basically unhappy in his life. When a series of events occurred that gave him a chance to be somebody else, he kept the card."

"Everybody'd like to be somebody else," said Ratso. "But forging a fake identity is rarely successful in civilian life. I imagine in the military it would be damn near impossible."

"Damn near impossible, my dear Watson, is not to say impossible. And besides, we must dream the impossible dream, Watson. We must fight the unbeatable foe—"

"Fuck the impossible dream," said Baker. "Exactly how did Tim fool the mighty military bureaucracy into thinking he was Luther Tibbs?"

"The answer is so simple," I said, "even a child could do it. In fact, a child *did* do it. I watched the child do it and I realized how Tim almost got away with it."

Through a window of my mind I could see a little girl in a peach-colored dress waving to me as she disappeared around a corner. I could see her kneeling on the sidewalk between the white Maltese and a cute Yorkie with the heart of a lion.

"In order to better match the ribbons in their hair she

switched the collars on her two little dogs, along, of course, with their dog tags. Ironically, soldier's ID tags have also been called dog tags probably as far back as World War I. So here's what had to have happened. For whatever reason, Tim and Luther swapped dog tags, probably just so one or the other of them could get off the base to go to town. Something as simple as that. It's frowned upon, of course, and it's risky, but it's not uncommon for such a temporary exchange to occur.

"Then, while Tim's in town with Luther's dog tags, Luther is suddenly called up for a mission. During the mission he's shot down over some paddy field in no-man's-land, and by the time he's found, many months later, the tags are the only identifiable item on the crash site. Also a not uncommon occurrence.

"Meanwhile, Tim, aware that Luther will one day be buried along with his name, is fearful of telling the authorities the truth, and secretly begins to savor the prospect of taking on a totally new identity in life. He's already weary of his own identity and of the war itself and this opportunity pushes his ruthless, cunning, battle-shocked mind over the edge. In the months ahead he really starts cookin' on another planet. He frags two officers, goes AWOL, eventually winds up in New York, and, in an incredibly unfortunate twist of fate for him, runs smack into his grieving widow, who runs immediately to her amateur-detective boyfriend with the news. Or maybe he was shadowing her all along. We'll probably never know. Either way, Tim knows what he's got to do. It's just like old times for him. Like night maneuvers in Vietnam, he pursues Judy and myself through the urban jungle of New York. To him, we are the enemy. He has to take us out or his position will be exposed. And there's not much doubt he would've fragged both of us, too. The only thing that finally stopped him, in fact, was a little girl in a peach-colored dress."

Though Ratso and the Bakerman were duly impressed with my explanation, the narrative itself, coupled with the events of the last few months, had tired me. I lay down for a much-needed power nap on the old skid-marked couch as the two of them headed for the door.

"Great work, Sherlock," said Ratso. "Get some rest before another big case crops up. And remember, that little girl was just playing with her dogs. You're the one who put it all together and found the solution."

"Thanks, Watson," I said. "Your third-degree black belt in sycophancy should be coming in any day now."

As I drifted off to sleep, the last words I remember were Tom Baker's.

"Brilliant piece of work, old bean," he said. "I'm proud of you, Dinky. I mean Stinky. I mean Pinky. I mean Finky. I mean *Kinky.*"

PART THREE The Future Tedious

The future is merely a necklace of nows.

Dennis Michael McKenna, September 29, 1945—June 15, 1993

46

I woke up on a cold floor with a hell of a headache, surrounded by mounds of chalky white dust and large white rocks. It looked like a marching-powder train had tipped over and trapped me underneath it. At first, it didn't seem like a bad way to go, but I tasted some of the powder and it didn't appear to give me much of a buzz. The next thing I knew two little dogs began ice-picking my brain with their loud barking. Somewhere between the two dogs stood a tall, beautiful, blond woman who for some reason looked vaguely familiar. The afternoon sunlight was streaming through her hair.

"The other painters loved the sunlight," I said, "but Van Gogh loved the sun. Where am I?"

"You're in your loft, hummingbird dick," she said. "Some plaster from the lesbian dance class must've collapsed on your head."

"What?" I said. I was still a little groggy. It felt like I'd been sleeping for twenty years. The two dogs yipping and yapping weren't really helping things either.

"Pyramus! Thisbe!" she said in a stern yet somehow sweet voice. "Shut up, darlings. You're bothering your sick Uncle Kinky."

"Where's the cat?" I asked, finally managing to rise to a sitting position.

"It'd probably be eating your body if the chicks and I hadn't found a way to get from the fire escape to the kitchen window. You said you were coming upstairs, then you never showed. Your phone was off the hook, so the girls and I went exploring and found you lying here in this mess. Don't you have a maid?"

Things were coming back to me now. This was my loft, all right. The gorgeous creature standing in front of me in very tall red stilettoes and a very short red dress was Stephanie DuPont. The view, I must say, was better than you usually get in New York.

"Where's the cat?" I said again.

"Around," said Stephanie casually. "I think the *enfants* chased her into the bedroom. Do you want a drink?"

"Do fish fart under water?" I said. "How long have I been out of it?"

"You've been out of it for about fifty-three years, dickhead," she said. "You've been passed out on the floor here for about two hours."

"Incredible," I said.

"I can think of a few other words for it," said Stephanie. "One of them is 'pathetic.'"

"What about the seven million dollars?" I asked. "You said

you had seven million dollars for me and I was on the way up to your place and something happened to me on the stairs."

"Something happened to you right here," she said. "A bunch of dancing dykes knocked some plaster on your head. You never even got to the stairs. And as for me giving you seven million dollars, you really must be dreaming! *You* might try to give *me* seven million dollars some day, but from the looks of things I rather doubt it. Your liquor cabinet is empty, as usual. I'll run upstairs and get you a brandy. We'll use the door this time. Don't worry. We'll be right back."

As I watched Stephanie and the two little dogs head for the door, I saw another young girl wave to me from the corner of my eye.

"Good-bye, Stephanie," I said. "Good-bye, Holly and Dandelion."

Stephanie stopped in her tracks. For the first time since I'd known her she actually seemed flustered.

"How could you know that?" she asked, looking suddenly rather shaky in her stilettoes. "I don't remember *ever* telling you that."

I just sat there in the dust smiling up at her, smiling up at the ruined ceiling, smiling up at the crazy, screwed-up world.

"Ah, my dear," I said, as gently as possible, "then you must have forgotten."

Epilogue

A bit of time has passed and I'm now pretty much back to my senses. The mind is a funny little thing and God knows where it can sometimes take us. The events in this book were not a dream. Some of them happened and some of them didn't. But the people of the book are very real.

Tom Baker went to Jesus in 1982, leaving my heart a lonelier place. Abbie Hoffman stepped on a rainbow in 1989, and everytime I question authority I think of him. Earl Buckelew rode off into the sunset this past year. I sang "Keep on the Sunnyside" at his funeral and I sure will, Earl.

As far as the Village Irregulars go, at this writing, they are all still very much alive. Larry "Ratso" Sloman, Mike McGovern, Steve Rambam, Chinga Chavin, Pete Myers, Mick Brennan, Piers Akerman, Ted Mann, Ross Waby, Cleve Hattersley, Mort Cooperman, Buddy Fox, Bill Dick, Winnie Katz, and the mildly mysterious Judy all continue, as I do, to sometimes stalk the valley of ennui known as Manhattan.

As for Stephanie DuPont, she remains quite tenacious about haunting my dreams and my life. She's brilliant, gorgeous, and sophisticated, but, as I occasionally point out to her, she still has a little growing up to do.

The cat, of course, will always be there. Walking across the pages of my life with awkward grace, saying nothing. Like Earl Buckelew's land, all she does is hold the world together.